Ghost Story

First published in Australia by South Coast Publishing, October 2014.
Copyright K.J. Emrick (2014)

This is a work of fiction. The characters, incidents and locations portrayed in this book and the names herein are fictitious. Any similarity to or identification with the locations, names, characters or history of any person, product or entity is entirely coincidental and unintentional.

- From a Declaration of Principles jointly adopted by a Committee of the American Bar Association and a Committee of Publishers and Associations.

All rights reserved. No part of this publication may be reproduced or transmitted in any form or by any means, electronic or mechanical, including photocopy, recording, or any information storage or retrieval system, without permission in writing from the publisher.

No responsibility or liability is assumed by the Publisher for any injury, damage or financial loss sustained to persons or property from the use of this information, personal or otherwise, either directly or indirectly. While every effort has been made to ensure reliability and accuracy of the information within, all liability, negligence or otherwise, from any use, misuse or abuse of the operation of any methods, strategies, instructions or ideas contained in the material herein, is the sole responsibility of the reader. Any copyrights not held by publisher are owned by their respective authors.

All information is generalized, presented for informational purposes only and presented "as is" without warranty or guarantee of any kind.

All trademarks and brands referred to in this book are for illustrative purposes only, are the property of their respective owners and not affiliated with this publication in any way. Any trademarks are being used without permission, and the publication of the trademark is not authorized by, associated with or sponsored by the trademark owner.

ISBN: 1507643292
ISBN-13: 9781507643297

Ghost Story

A DARCY SWEET COZY MYSTERY

K. J. EMRICK

Chapter One

Lying on her bed flipping through the pages of a calendar, Darcy Sweet slashed another red X through another square. Never in her life had she been so worried about what day of the week was which.

She flipped through the months now, each page covered with their notes and question marks for maybes or slashing red lines for definite no's. "Which one of us said that picking a date would be fun?" she asked, kicking her feet in the air as she rolled from her back over to her belly.

"That was you," Jon told her, sitting on the edge of the mattress with a calendar of his own. He was in his jeans and an old white t-shirt, his usual clothes for a day off. Darcy had put on shorts and her favorite purple tank top to dive into this project. A casual day with her fiancé was not to be wasted.

"There's always Valentine's Day," he suggested for the fifth time.

"Ugh, too cliché," she said.

"Are we sure you don't just want to elope?"

Jon Tinker, the love of Darcy's life and her very patient fiancé, laid across the bed next to her and began tickling her neck with soft kisses, pulling aside her long dark hair and making her shiver.

"Jon, I'm serious. We need to pick a date for—"

She broke off in a squeal as he found that spot on her side with his fingers where he knew she was super sensitive. She had no choice but to defend herself, and it wasn't long before they were tangled up in the sheets and with each other. His soft lips were stealing her breath away as he kissed her over and over. Her bare feet tickled his. Playful touches became flirtatious, and Darcy began to think they were never going to get around to picking a day.

They had been at this all morning. Choosing a date from the calendar, not flirting with each other. Although, that *had* taken up a lot of their time. After wishing over and over for a day to just relax with Jon, it had finally happened on this fine morning one day in October. Neither of them had to go to work. There were no weird murders or mysterious events for either of them to investigate. No ghosts were hovering around Darcy trying to get her attention.

It had been over two weeks, actually, since she had seen any ghost at all. Except for her Great Aunt Millie down at the bookstore. She was always there. Other than her, nothing. The lack of spiritual activity was strange for Misty Hollow. Even stranger for Darcy herself. She'd been seeing and talking to ghosts since, well, puberty. Not seeing any at all for two weeks almost felt like she'd lost the hearing in one ear, or lost the ability to taste grape jelly.

Well. Something like that.

Jon's strong and muscular body felt good wrapped around her. Darcy feathered her hands into his black hair and pinned him down by rolling over, sitting across his chest, victorious. "Ha! I win!"

"I let you win, you know." When she looked at him skeptically he added, "No, really. I'm still worried about your arm."

GHOST STORY

Darcy twisted her lips and flexed her left arm for him. The nerve had been pinched there just last month by a man Darcy hoped to never meet again. Ever. It had been completely numb for days and it had taken even longer for her to get any kind of strength back in it, but it was fine now.

"Whatever," she told him, sticking out her tongue. "You know I won."

"I could let you win every day for the rest of our lives," he said with a wry smile, "if it means keeping you in bed with me."

She smacked the palm of her hand gently against his chest. "For Pete's sake, Jon, that's what we're trying to figure out. The rest of our lives has to start sometime. Now help me pick a date for our wedding!"

Catching her wrists he pulled her down closer to him. "We'll pick the perfect date," he told her, "but the rest of our lives started the moment you agreed to marry me. Our wedding is just the icing on that cake. I love you, Darcy."

She wanted to tell him how much she loved him, too, especially when he let his tough-guy guard down and said things like that. The words couldn't get past the sudden lump in her throat. Her heart swelled. She loved him more in that moment than she had at any time before in their complicated relationship.

It wasn't complicated anymore. They were getting married. Someday.

Okay, so still a little complicated.

At least now she knew that someday would come. There was no doubt for either of them now. They wanted to be with each other. Knowing that made everything perfect. Nothing could ruin this moment.

Into that thought, the phone on the bedside table rang.

Darcy bit her lip and sheepishly lowered her forehead to rest against Jon's shoulder. He put his hands gently around her heart-shaped face and lifted her eyes to his. "You were thinking it, weren't you?"

She nodded, miserably, twisting the antique silver ring on her right hand like she did whenever she got nervous. "I didn't mean to!"

Jon laughed, and hugged her like it didn't really matter, but both of them knew the rule. You never said or thought or whispered to yourself how nothing could go wrong. The Universe hated it when you said things like that, and the Universe was always listening, ready to pounce and prove you wrong.

"Way to go," Jon teased, still laughing. "Now the world's going to end."

"Jon!" she scolded him, rolling away as he sat up. "Don't say that!"

"Why not? I can't jinx it any more than you already did." He winked to let her know he wasn't really mad and then reached over on his side of the bed where the phone sat in its recharging base. It was on its fourth ring as he picked it up. "I'm going to change your nickname to Jinx."

"Uh-uh," she said quickly. "I like the nickname you have for me now."

He blew her a kiss, and she caught it out of the air, as he pushed the answer button. "Hello? Oh, hi Helen. What can I do for the town's mayor?"

Darcy stretched, appreciating the way Jon watched her from the corner of his eye as she did. Helen Nelson had been keeping to herself a lot lately. She hadn't been at the bakery she owned in town. Darcy hadn't seen her walking around the streets of misty Hollow like she usually did, either. Darcy wondered what could have prompted her to call out of the blue like this. Maybe she wanted Jon to do something for her in his capacity as the police department's Chief Detective.

"Sure," she heard Jon saying. "What time is it now?"

He looked past Darcy to her side of the room, where the digital alarm clock sat on Darcy's dresser. It was already quarter to eleven in the morning.

"Sure, lunch is fine," he told Helen. "Where? Oh. All right. That would be great. Should we bring anything?"

Darcy blinked at him. "We?" she asked in a whisper.

Jon shrugged, still talking into the phone. "All right, Helen. Thanks. We'll be there."

Leaning over again he put the phone back into its base. Then he shifted over to where Darcy was and kissed her nose. "Helen just invited us to lunch."

"Really?" Darcy and Helen, and Jon too of course, were good friends but Darcy hadn't been over to Helen's house since her husband had been arrested for murder and embezzling town funds. Darcy had been the main reason Steve had been arrested, and it had always been just a little too awkward ever since then to go over to Helen's house. Helen didn't hold it against her, of course, but Darcy couldn't help but remember how Steve had tried to kill her. It meant a lot that Helen would call them up to lunch now.

Jon threw the blankets aside and swung his feet out to the floor. "Let's get showered," he suggested. "I think we should pick up a cake or something for dessert."

"Hey, wait a minute," Darcy complained, wrapping her arms around him and pulling him back to her. "I'm not ready to go. Not just yet."

Misty Hollow had been painted with an artist's pallet of reds and yellows and oranges. The trees surrounding the town always put on an impressive show for autumn. A number of out-of-towners had checked into McQuaid's Motor Inn out on Fairbanks Road for the season, but the nearby town of Oak Hollow was the more popular tourist attraction in the area.

Jon drove slower than he needed to as they made their way to Helen's house so they could enjoy the view, too. Darcy loved this time of year. She wondered if she and Jon could find a day or two to go back up to the cabins at Bear Ridge to go hiking before the weather turned cold. The mayor there had extended the use of the ski lodges whenever they wanted in thanks for their role in bringing a serial killer to justice.

Her life brought her to some very strange places and events, to be sure, but it wasn't all bad. After all, it had brought Jon into her life.

They had picked up a cheesecake with blueberry topping from Helen's own bakery before heading over to her house. Darcy knew her friend wouldn't mind. She'd seen Helen shopping there herself. There was no denying the excellence Helen put into her business.

Pulling away from the curb in front of the bakery, they had started down Main Street and were enjoying the scenery of their sleepy little town when Darcy turned to Jon to say something to him, and froze.

Jon noticed the look on her face, the way she stared at him with her mouth half open. "Hey. What is it?"

"I…don't know." Had she been about to say something? There had been a thought in her head but it was gone now. "I guess not."

There was a pressure building at the back of her skull like a migraine headache. Like something was steadily pushing against her mind. She smiled at Jon, trying to pretend everything was all right, but couldn't hold his gaze. Instead, she turned to look out the window.

The Town Hall stared back at her.

Darcy jumped in her seat, startled. For just a moment, the red brick building with its triangular entryway roof and stopped clock really had looked like it was watching her. There was just a brief impression of a face, a man's face, regarding her with cold menace.

For all of her adult life, Darcy had been able to tap into abilities that most people had only heard about in movies or those paranormal mystery books. She could see the world of ghosts, communicate with the dearly departed, even call upon the dead for advice with techniques that her Great Aunt Millie had taught her. It had been a lot to handle at times. That wasn't the half of it, though.

She could sense things. She could know things that her normal five senses couldn't tell her. It was almost like she had been born with a sixth sense, something that had been passed down to her through the family genes.

Right now, her sixth sense was screaming at her.

For the last few months now Darcy had been sensing a presence in the Town Hall. A presence that had gotten stronger, and stronger. That was nothing uncommon for Darcy. She knew where several spirits lived right here in town…if that was the correct term. They didn't exactly live anywhere, really, since they were dead. Aunt Millie's ghost resided in the bookstore that Darcy had inherited from her after she died. There were two young children in the graveyard in town who had never moved on from the place they were buried. For some reason a woman's ghost kept trying to rake the leaves under one particular tree in the park. There were maybe half a dozen others who hadn't been able to move on to the next realm still trapped here in town.

None of them frightened Darcy. This one in the Town Hall did.

Months ago she had stumbled onto a story in an old book about the Pilgrim Ghost. A man named Nathaniel Williams was said to haunt the Misty Hollow Town Hall. He had been hung as a witch back in the 1700s, and Darcy could see where a thing like that would make a spirit restless. The story in the book had never seemed very real to Darcy. She had been in the Town Hall any number of times and not felt or sensed anything.

Until recently. Something was definitely there. Maybe it had been hiding, or maybe it only showed up at certain times. Darcy didn't know, but it had appeared slowly and then grown stronger over a period of weeks. A presence that watched her whenever she stepped inside. It was beginning to freak her out. Seeing that skeletal face that had been superimposed over the façade of the Town Hall for just a split second, she figured she had a right to be bothered.

Not just bothered. Scared.

There was something different about that ghost. It seemed to be carrying some kind of grudge. Every time she went inside the Town Hall it would be there, stalking her, angrily breathing down her neck. Figuratively speaking, of course. Now it seemed to be reaching out to brush her with its angry presence even when she was just close to the building.

Just once, she'd like it if her sixth sense attracted the ghost of Walt Disney. Or someone famous from history.

Was this the Pilgrim Ghost from the story? Possibly. The story hadn't said anything about that ghost being hostile. Just that people had seen objects move around or heard strange noises. Nothing as serious as what Darcy had seen and felt. This ghost needed to be investigated, and she'd promised herself to do exactly that more than once but there always seemed to be something else in the way. Whether it was murderers or kidnappers or just her own life, there was always something.

Now might just be a good time to finally look into the history of the Town Hall and of Misty Hollow itself and see if she could at least figure out for certain who this ghost was. After all, it was the time of year for it. Late October, almost Halloween.

She shivered and made herself look forward out the windshield again. An image of Ichabod Crane and the Headless Horseman had flashed through her mind. Poor Ichabod had been killed by a ghost when he thought he was safe. That wouldn't happen here. This ghost couldn't hurt her. It could try its scare tactics all it wanted. She knew better. Only the strongest of spirits could affect the world of the living. Poltergeist activity was the most that Darcy had ever seen. Objects thrown around a room, blasts of air, ghostly screams. That sort of thing. She'd read in her Aunt Millie's journals about ghosts who could do more, do far worse, but she'd never seen anything like that—

"Darcy?"

She shifted in her seat, twisting her aunt's antique ring furiously around her finger. "Sorry, Jon. I guess I got distracted."

His hand reached for hers and held it tight. "You look like you're worried about something. Anything I should know about?"

"Just the usual," she told him.

The look on his face changed to one of patient understanding. Jon knew all about her abilities and the messes they got her into. More than once those same abilities had solved mysteries ranging from murder to kidnapping, but they had gotten in the way of their relationship on more than one occasion, too. Not that he didn't have a few skeletons in his own closet, but hers would always trump his. Hands down.

She leaned over and cozied up to him, shoulder to shoulder, holding his hand up to her lips as he drove slowly and carefully with the other on the wheel. "Don't worry, Jon. I'm not planning on getting us involved in any big mysteries. Not today, anyway."

"I love you." That wasn't exactly him saying that he believed her. "I know you don't ever mean to get involved in things. Trouble just has a way of finding you."

"Um, you too, as I recall."

"Sure, sure. But usually it's you."

Darcy started to argue that point but realized she couldn't. "Fair enough. How about I cross my heart and promise not to get involved in any mystery solving today?"

"Deal," he said quickly, before she could take it back. "We'll just have a nice, quiet lunch with our friends and then we'll get back to planning that special day of ours."

She settled down against him again, happy to be talking about normal, everyday life things. Her mother had just gotten remarried. Just last month her sister Grace had given birth to Darcy's first niece. Darcy thought she was past due to have a little normal in her own life.

A few more turns brought them to a short side street where Helen's sprawling two story mansion sat on three acres of land. Helen came from one of the founding families of Misty Hollow and the house and the land both had been passed down through the generations to her. Darcy's family was one of the older families here, too. People tended to stay in Misty Hollow. It was just that kind of place.

Ghost Story

Helen put a lot of pride into her family home. Hedgerows marked the edges of the property line. Lower shrubs with purplish flowers budding all over them had been trimmed to evenly flat tops, and then behind those was a row of ones taller than Darcy that sprouted white blossoms. Flowers had been planted artistically in circular patterns up closer to the house in autumn colors of orange and yellow. In the middle of the lawn a ceramic birdbath jetted a fountain of water from its center. A little pretentious for Darcy, but very pretty.

The house had been recently repainted a light blue with a white trim around the doors and windows. The last time Darcy had been here the whole thing had been white. After her husband had been arrested and sent to prison, Helen had apparently wanted a change. Somehow that little difference made coming here that much easier.

"Hey, look who else is here," Jon said to her, pointing at the driveway.

A yellow sedan was parked up near the house. Darcy recognized it immediately as the one Grace and Aaron had only just bought. Darcy made fun of her sister for buying something so practical, but Grace had only growled at her and said she had to think of her baby now.

"I didn't realize Helen was inviting them, too." Darcy wondered what Helen might have up her sleeve. She knew that she and her boyfriend Andrew Lansky had been dating for a few months now but she doubted they would have any big announcement to share. Not this soon. It was always possible that she had just wanted to have a get-together with friends, but just out of the blue like this?

"I guess it's going to be a real party." Jon shrugged. "Maybe I should have worn something besides jeans."

"I like you in your jeans," Darcy said as they parked behind Grace's car. "I hardly ever get to see you dress down. Besides, I'm in my jeans too."

"Sure, but you look better in yours than I do in mine."

"Oh, I don't know about that," Darcy said coyly. "Come on. We can ask my sister who looks better."

They were both laughing as they got out and went up to ring the front doorbell. Jon balanced the cake box in the crook of his left arm, and they waited.

A middle aged man answered the door to them with a smile. His hair was dark and thick and Darcy was fairly certain that it was still its natural color. He was wearing a baker's apron with the words "Bean There Bakery and Café" printed on the front, over a comfortable flannel shirt and dark blue slacks. Helen's boyfriend seemed very comfortable in her house, Darcy thought to herself.

"Hi there, guys," Andrew greeted them. "Come on in. I've got everything ready and Helen's just putting it out on the table now."

"Thanks Andrew." Darcy gave Andrew a quick kiss on his cheek. He'd been working at Helen's café for about eight months now and Darcy had gotten to know him pretty well. It was nice to see Helen had moved on after her divorce from Steve and could be happy again.

Jon shook Andrew's hand, still awkwardly holding the cheesecake. "Uh, maybe you should take this," he said, offering the box to Andrew.

"Ah, excellent!" Andrew said as he caught sight of the logo on the cake box. "Helen likes it when her friends shop at her bakery. What kind did you get?"

"Blueberry cheesecake," Jon told him. "Hope that's all right?"

"Definitely. It's one of my favorites, I know that. Grace and Aaron brought a lemon meringue with them so we'll have plenty of dessert for after lunch."

"We could have brought more with us if you guys had let us know you were planning a lunch party," Darcy said, sliding her feet out of her sneakers to leave them at the door. Helen had carpeting through most of her house and she liked to keep them clean.

Jon did the same with his shoes. "Why did she decide to have us over, anyway?" he asked. "What's the occasion?"

Andrew shifted his weight and his smile turned a little sheepish. "I'm not really sure. We went to bed last night after watching a movie and she didn't say anything about it at all. Then this morning she woke up insisting that I start cooking a lunch for all of us." He shrugged. "I try not to ask questions when she gets an idea in her head. You know how insistent she can be."

It hadn't escaped Darcy's attention that Andrew had spent the night here with Helen. Apparently their relationship had gotten more serious than she realized. Good for Helen, she thought to herself. Still, it was odd to just wake up and decide to have a lunch party on the spur of the moment.

Andrew excused himself back to the kitchen, telling them that everyone else was in the dining room already. Jon turned to Darcy and took her by the hand. "Stop it," he whispered.

"What do you mean?"

"I know that look on your face. I can almost see the wheels turning in your mind. This is just a lunch. Nothing mysterious about it at all. Don't go looking for trouble where there isn't any. We get enough of it all on our own without having to do that."

Feeling silly, Darcy rolled her eyes and squeezed Jon's hand. "I know. Sorry, I guess I just can't help myself."

He kissed her forehead and pulled her after him down to the dining room. "That's just one of the many reasons why I love you, Darcy Sweet."

Chapter Two

"Hey, sis." Grace waved with one hand from where she sat at the dinner table.

Darcy loved seeing Grace this way. Motherhood definitely agreed with her. She had her feet kicked out in front of her and her arm protectively around the baby sleeping soundly in the sling carrier she wore over one shoulder and across her chest. She was letting her dark hair grow long again and she was more relaxed than Darcy could remember seeing her in a very long time.

The fact that she hadn't gotten back to work at the police department didn't even make her upset anymore. Her life, for the moment, revolved around her baby and the family she had started with Aaron.

Darcy's brother-in-law stood behind Grace, hands massaging her shoulders, already completely at ease in his role as a father. The baby had been unplanned, but neither of them would want it any other way. Little Addison Darcy Wentworth would always have a lot of love in her life.

The little baby girl was asleep, lulled by the warmth of her mother's body and the sound of her heartbeat, and Darcy was careful not to wake her as she gently pulled back the soft blue fabric of the sling to get a better look at her adorable face. "I think she's going to look just like you, Grace."

"Better her than me," Aaron agreed. "If she grows up beautiful like her mom then I figure I've done something right."

"Looks like you did something right already," Jon told him, clapping him on the shoulder.

Darcy looked up at Jon with a smile. He would never know it, but sometimes he had a knack for saying just the right thing at just the right time.

"How's my replacement doing?" Grace asked Jon. "I hope you didn't give him my desk."

"Of course not." Jon shook his head and sat down across the table from her. "Wilson isn't your replacement. Chief Daleson is going to keep three detectives from now on. You, me, and Wilson. He's doing all right. I have to coach him through a few things but for the most part he knows his stuff. Of course, his new girlfriend is taking up a lot of his time."

A sad smile crossed Darcy's face. She couldn't help it. Wilson's new girlfriend was actually his old girlfriend from back when they were both in school. Lindsay had run off and gotten married to someone else and then come back to Misty Hollow only to have her husband killed. Now, with the killer behind bars, Wilson had been spending a lot of time with Lindsay and their relationship had rekindled. It was nice to see something good come from that tragedy.

"So where's our hostess?" Jon was asking. He waved a hand to indicate the dining table already set with plates and spoons and forks and knives, pink cloth napkins folded just so next to each setting, a small bouquet of late season flowers in the very center. "The only thing missing is the food. And Helen."

Ghost Story

"Here's both!" Helen called out with a little chuckle, pushing her way through the swinging saloon-style doors that separated the dining area from the kitchen. She was holding a blue ceramic cooking pot by the side handles, both of her hands inside floral print oven mitts. She wore the same kind of apron that Andrew had, straight from her own café, over her blue dress. Her graying hair was tied into the ponytail she had taken to wearing all the time whenever she wasn't performing her duties as mayor.

Andrew appeared behind her with a large wooden bowl of salad in one hand and a smaller bowl of steaming rolls in the other. He and Helen shared a look between them that Darcy knew very well. It was the same look she and Jon had for each other.

The table was set and food was passed around. The main dish turned out to be a chicken stew of Helen's own recipe, tender grilled pieces of chicken in a gravy with carrots and pearl onions and tiny slivers of celery accompanied by hunks of biscuits worked right in with everything else. Darcy made a mental note to remind herself to get the recipe later. Not that she was any kind of cook. She'd inherited her mother's gene when it came to cooking. But maybe she could get Jon to make this for them sometimes. He seemed to do better than she with the cooking related chores.

Small talk ranged from the current cases Jon was working on, to the construction of the new dollar store set to begin in the spring, to the weather, and of course Grace's baby. Wine was served with the meal. Darcy noticed how Jon made sure to only have a few sips from his glass before drinking water. He was driving, after all.

Finally, salads and bread and awesome chicken stew devoured, Helen clapped her hands together and declared that she hoped everyone had saved enough room for dessert.

"Oh, Helen," Aaron said, patting his belly. "I don't know. That third helping of stew really did me in."

"Nonsense, Aaron," Helen teased him. "You've got plenty of room there. I, for one, can't wait to try that cheesecake you and Jon brought, Darcy. I think Elizabeth made that, and she is such a wonderful baker. That was one of the reasons I hired her, you know."

Getting up from where he sat next to Helen at the head of the table, Andrew leaned over and kissed her cheek. "So why did you hire me?"

"I thought you looked cute in an apron," was her answer. Andrew rewarded her with another kiss.

Jon quirked an eyebrow at Darcy, with a smile to match. He liked seeing their friend happy, too. Darcy might have been the main reason Helen's ex-husband had been arrested for murder, but it was Jon and Grace who had made the arrest. If Andrew could make Helen happy again, that would ease a lot of bad memories for everyone.

"So," Andrew said to them, "I'll go and get the desserts ready to serve. Excuse me."

He headed off into the kitchen, the swinging doors slapping at each other as he passed through them. The conversation lagged a bit at that point. Everyone was full of good food, comfortable in their silence.

Helen began humming to herself, nodding her head every so often, staring down at the table. She picked up the cloth napkin from her plate and began twisting it back and forth in her hands.

Ghost Story

Across from Darcy, Addison began to fuss and stir in her carrier. Grace rocked her back and forth gently and cooed softly until the baby settled again.

"Thanks again for the invitation," Jon said to Helen. "What made you decide to have a party?"

She looked up, her eyes going through Jon for just a moment before focusing again. "Oh. I, uh, needed to talk to all of you. All of you. You need to know."

"Hm?" Jon said, confused. He leaned forward in his chair, looking at Darcy and Grace and Aaron to see if maybe they knew what Helen had meant. "You need to tell us something? Is it serious?"

"Yes."

Darcy noticed the faraway tone in Helen's voice. Her eyes lost their focus again. It was like their friend was here at the dinner table in her house with them, but at the same time, she wasn't.

Addison fussed again, making little upset baby noises in her sleep.

"Helen, what's wrong?" Jon asked her. He was sitting on Darcy's left, closest to Helen, and he reached out like he was going to shake her awake.

She pulled back into herself, crossing her arms over her chest, hugging her shoulders. Blinking rapidly, shaking all over, she twisted her head back and forth, back and forth. "No. No, no, no. No, he wants me to tell you. You need to know."

"Helen?" Andrew had come back in from the kitchen, glass serving trays holding perfectly sliced pieces of cheesecake and lemon meringue pie. He hesitated, sensing that something had happened in his absence but not knowing what. "Is something wrong?"

Helen's chair crashed loudly to the floor as she sprang up to her feet and turned on Andrew, arm extended, her finger pointing accusingly. "You!"

Andrew took a step back from her. Jon and Aaron both got up from their chairs slowly.

Addison cried out, once, and then began pushing with all of her infant strength against the sling.

Helen swung back to the table and Darcy saw the way her face had gone slack. There was no emotion there at all. None. Her lips pulled back from her teeth harshly. Her eyes rolled back into her head.

And she spoke to them.

"You! All of you! Listen to me. The spirit of Nathaniel Williams commands you to listen! You have taken for yourselves that which is mine!"

Nathaniel Williams. Darcy couldn't believe what she was hearing. The Pilgrim Ghost. Helen was talking about the Pilgrim Ghost.

No. Not talking about him. Talking like she was him. Her voice had changed. It was more masculine, stronger, and there was a strange accent layered over the words. Not quite British. That wasn't Helen's voice.

"Darcy…?" Jon said slowly, keeping his eyes on Helen.

"I know. It's not Helen." Darcy understood why Jon had asked her for an explanation. He knew when things had taken a turn into the weird, and Darcy was the expert on all things bizarre and strange.

Something else was controlling Helen.

She was possessed.

Make it stop, came the words in Darcy's mind. *Make her stop. I'm scared!*

Ghost Story

Darcy couldn't place the source of the whispered plea. She thought at first it was Helen, connecting with her somehow through Darcy's sixth sense. That wasn't it, though. She could feel the speaker in her mind, could sense them, and it didn't feel like Helen. It was the feeling of someone very, very young. Someone Innocent.

Mouth falling open, she looked down at Addison in her mother's arms.

"One of you will pay!" Helen demanded in that other voice, slamming the flat of her hand down on the table, yanking Darcy's attention back. Saliva drooled out of the corner of Helen's mouth. "One of you will be my tool. My weapon. I will hold you in my hand and I will use you to take my town back. It shall be mine once more!"

Not wasting any time on how impossibly crazy this all seemed, Darcy stood up, standing close to Jon. They were depending on her. Everyone, including Helen. No one else knew how to relate to spirits. "You are the ghost of Nathaniel Williams?" she asked, her mouth dry.

"Aye," Helen answered in the ghost's voice. "I am he. You are trespassers. This land is and always has been mine. All of you will leave, down to the last woman and child, or else you will suffer. Suffer!" The ghost added a special emphasis on that word, wracking Helen's body into a hard spasm. The sight of it twisted Darcy's stomach in knots.

"How?" she made herself ask. "How will we pay, Nathaniel? Tell us what you want."

"I want you to leave!" Helen shrieked. Her fingers clawed at the table, digging into the wood, leaving trails of her blood as she tore her nails. "You will leave my town, leave me alone, or you will pay the price!"

"Okay," Darcy said, wanting to keep the ghost calm, wanting to keep him talking, but scared for what this conversation might be doing to Helen. "All right, Nathaniel. We're listening. Tell me how we will pay. How will we suffer?"

Darcy, please, make her stop!

The force of a tidal wave built up in Darcy's brain and she was suddenly doubled over, holding onto the edge of the table for dear life, the nice meal she had just eaten rising up in her gorge. She grabbed on to the back of Jon's chair with both hands and made herself stay in control.

"How, Nathaniel? How will we pay?" Darcy had to raise her voice to be heard over the roar in her ears.

She saw Jon and Aaron down on their knees, Aaron holding his head in his hands, Jon clutching his throat like he couldn't breathe.

"Tell us how!"

Grace huddled protectively over Addison as her baby screamed and cried and shouted in the background of Darcy's thoughts.

Into that ballooning pressure Helen drove words like spikes. "ONE OF YOU WILL BE CONDEMNED TO KILL!"

Darcy's ears popped and her mind exploded into buzzing silence, and everything went black.

⁓

"Darcy? Darcy, wake up."

She did, but she regretted it.

When she had been asleep, blissfully unaware of anything around her, she hadn't felt the hammer blows her pulse kept striking against the inside of her skull. She sure felt them now.

Ghost Story

"Ow," she said. "Ow. Ow."

"There you are." Jon smiled down at her as she opened her eyes. She was on the floor, looking up, and he was kneeling over her. A dinner table was next to them. She could see where plates and glasses and trays of desserts had fallen, scattering everywhere. Oh. Oh that's right, she thought. We were at Helen's for lunch, and she…

"Where's Helen? Is she—?" She broke off midsentence as she snapped herself up into a sitting position and nearly passed out all over again. Stars swam in front of her eyes. Her stomach rose and then fell and then rose again. "Oh, that does not feel good."

"Tell me about it, sis," Grace said. She was sitting up, on the floor as well, and Darcy could see her through the legs of the table holding Addison, who had somehow managed to fall back asleep, curled up into her mother like nothing had happened at all. "What just happened?"

"I'm not sure," Darcy answered truthfully. Had she really been listening to baby Addison's thoughts before? Was that even possible? She rubbed her temples and decided that she should only tackle one impossible thing at a time. "Jon, where's Helen?"

"I'm right here," Helen said, sitting up in her place at the head of the table, her chair turned upright again. Her hands trembled as she held them in front of her, several of the nails broken ragged and bleeding. Blood had smeared down her arms. Andrew was kneeling next to her, holding a small wastebasket lined with a plastic bag. From the smell, Darcy figured Helen had used it a couple of times already. "I mean, I'm here now. Darcy," she whispered, "what was that?"

"It was a ghost," Darcy said. "That much I'm sure of."

"How?" Helen looked like she was about to be violently sick again and Andrew moved the bucket closer. "Oh, Dear God, what's going on?"

Darcy had seen possessions before. They weren't always pleasant for the person being possessed but she didn't remember ever seeing an event this powerful. The ghost had forced its presence on all of them, like a velvet glove reaching in to squeeze their brains. Darcy's head felt like it had been wrung through a juicer.

"Does your head hurt like this?" she asked Jon.

"Yes," he said in a quiet voice that didn't carry past her ears. "That was completely freaky, Darcy. Can you answer Helen's question? Do you know what just happened?"

She felt like reminding him that he was the detective, but they both knew this was her area of expertise. "I'll need to check on a few things. That ghost…I've felt that presence before. That spirit. In the Town Hall. It's the one I've been telling you about from the Town Hall."

"The Pilgrim's Ghost? The one that's been making you avoid the place like the plague?"

She opened her mouth to argue with him that she hadn't been doing that but really, he was right. She could have investigated that haunting long before now. All of her excuses about not having time really only meant one thing. She was afraid. Afraid like she'd never been before in her life.

"I know this much," she said, "that ghost really, really needed to talk to us if it was able to hijack Helen's body to do it. That kind of means a very strong entity."

He eyed her, and she realized why. She'd called this spirit an entity. Not a ghost, not a soul, not the dearly departed. Entity. It had a very negative and menacing connotation to it. Darcy hadn't used that word on purpose, but it fit perfectly with what she had just felt.

"Oh, come on, Darcy," Andrew said angrily. "You would skip right to possession. Don't you think that just maybe my Helen is stressed or tired or something?"

Darcy didn't try to argue with him. Very few of the people in town believed her when she talked about these things. It didn't matter if the evidence was right in front of them. It didn't matter what Andrew had just seen or experienced. He wanted an easy, understandable answer.

"Andrew, hush," Helen said gently. She let him lean her head against his shoulder. Her color looked better, to Darcy's eyes, but she was obviously drained by what the possession had done to her.

Jon didn't try to argue with Andrew, either. "What concerns me is what you said at the end there. Helen, could you hear yourself?"

She shook her head no, curling her hand into the front of Andrew's shirt for comfort. "I could see everything, but it was all blurry, and there was just this violent ringing noise in my ears."

"You said...um." It was Andrew who started to answer. He faltered and then drew a shaky breath and tried again. "You said that one of us will be condemned to kill."

She looked up into his eyes, then over at Darcy. "What does that mean?"

"Helen, I wish I knew. I just don't. Let me look into some things. There might be a way for me to contact this spirit without him, you know, using you to threaten your friends."

Helen sat up straighter, trying in the midst of an impossibly uncertain situation to look certain. She nodded her head curtly. "Thank you. That would be very helpful."

Getting back to her feet with Jon's help, Darcy looked around the room at each of them. "For now, I don't think we should tell anyone about this. All of you know a little bit of the things I can do. My gifts. You know that I use them to help people."

Grace's face was sour. Aaron's was blank, and Darcy imagined he was remembering the awful few days when he had been kidnapped and Darcy had used her gifts to help find him. Andrew averted his eyes. Helen's lip quivered.

When she looked at Jon, there was quiet encouragement in his eyes. He took her hand in his and held it tightly and it gave her the courage to go on. Knowing that he was with her no matter what they came up against made her feel stronger.

"Anyway," she continued after a deep breath, "I will figure this out. You just need to give me some time. And trust me, don't tell anyone, because they either won't believe us or they'll think we're crazy."

"I can see why," Andrew muttered.

Darcy ignored him. That was the typical reaction from "normal" people dealing with ghosts and the afterlife. Denial.

It didn't matter. Whatever Andrew wanted to believe or didn't want to believe didn't change the facts. They were dealing with a hostile entity—yes, entity—and if Darcy didn't figure out what to do about him there would be worse trouble than what they had just seen.

Trouble.

She remembered a vision her Great Aunt had sent her just a few weeks ago in a dream. Aunt Millie had warned Darcy that trouble was coming, and she'd been worried that Darcy might not be ready for it. In fact, Darcy had been scared to death by the look on her aunt's face.

If this was the trouble that Millie was warning her about, they were all in serious danger.

GHOST STORY

"Come on," Jon said to her. "We should get home. I imagine there's some book reading you'll want to do."

"Definitely." Darcy leaned on him for support. "Helen, I'm sorry this happened to you. I'll do everything I can to find out what's going on. Okay? I need to look into my aunt's books. Maybe she knew something that could help us."

She needed to look through the history books, too. Maybe rereading that story about the Pilgrim Ghost would help. There might have been some detail she missed. There had to be something else about Nathaniel Williams written down somewhere, didn't there? He thought Misty Hollow was his town. His name must be mentioned somewhere.

Grace and Aaron said their goodbyes as well, promising to keep in touch to make sure Helen was all right. Darcy took a moment to stroke baby Addison's cheek. Had she heard Addison's voice? Really? She didn't know, but she did know that Addison had been affected by the ghostly visitation just like the rest of them had. On such a young mind, that sort of thing could leave a lasting impression.

"What time is it?" Aaron asked, looking up at the clock in the entryway hall. "That can't be right. Can it?"

Darcy looked at the clock. It read several hours after what she thought it should have. Six o'clock. Some five hours later than what it had been just before Andrew had brought out those desserts. Where had that time gone?

"Did we all pass out?" Darcy asked. "All of us?"

"I know I did," Aaron said, checking his watch against the clock on the wall over and over. Grace and Jon and even Helen nodded that they had passed out, too.

So…all of them had passed out and lost five hours or more of their day. Darcy had never heard of anything like that, either in her aunt's journals or from any other source. How could that happen?

"I guess," Jon said, grumbling as he opened the front door to Helen's house, "that we're all lucky we're not…dead…"

Darcy saw it as soon as she stepped out onto the porch next to Jon. On the front lawn, surrounded by pretty flowers, with the bird bath bubbling away cheerfully, a body lay in the manicured grass. A woman, on her back, her hands crossed over her chest and her lifeless eyes staring at the clear sky above. Blood stained her white blouse across her stomach where multiple stab wounds had torn the fabric. Her hands and arms were stained red. Dark hair lay bunched beneath her head like a pillow. A blue skirt settled perfectly over her legs even though the left one had been broken below the knee, the foot twisted at an awkward angle and the femur bone sticking out through the flesh.

"Oh my God," Grace said, slowly. Aaron put his hands on her shoulders, his face pale.

"I'll call it in," Jon said, already digging into his jeans for his cell phone. "Aaron, go back inside with Helen and Andrew. Tell them to stay inside. Grace, go with them, okay?"

Darcy stared at the body. There was no sense in checking for a pulse or trying CPR. Death's pallor had already claimed whoever this was. A dead body. Here on the lawn. Dumped outside of the house while all of them had been passed out inside.

Or had they?

One of you will be condemned to kill, the ghost of Nathaniel Williams had warned them. Now here was death at their doorstep.

One of them was the murderer.

But…who?

GHOST STORY

She felt cold all over, and numb, and scared. What had happened here?

A shiver of movement caught Darcy's attention. Looking past the dead woman, over to the hedge rows with their colorful flowers, she saw tendrils of ground fog snaking their way out of the shadows. Mists, gathering and thickening as evening drew closer.

Trouble wasn't just coming to Misty Hollow. It had already found them.

Chapter Three

The six of them agreed to a simple story before anyone else showed up. They had been inside at a lunch party and didn't hear anything. They didn't discover the poor dead woman until they came outside to leave. Not all of them were happy with the idea of lying. Grace argued against it but Jon and Aaron were able to point out the problems with truthfully reporting that they had been attacked by a ghost who had possessed one or more of their group and then made one of them commit murder.

All of them were suspects now. They had to stick together until they could figure out what had really happened. It helped that there were exactly two other houses on this street, and no one had been home at either one. So. No witnesses.

Which was good and bad. On the one hand, it helped make their story sound more plausible since no one could contradict it. Then again, it would have been nice to talk to someone who had actually seen something. At least then Darcy would know where to start looking for clues.

Jon didn't like the idea of going back home and pretending their lives were normal but they really didn't have any other choice. Detective Wilson Barton had asked his questions and the uniformed officers had taken crime scene photos and collected their evidence and the woman's body had been taken away to the hospital over in Meadowood where an autopsy would tell them more. There was nothing left for the six of them to do.

Nothing, except figure out which one of them was a killer. That part would be up to Darcy.

She stifled a yawn behind the back of her hand and closed the book she had been reading. It went onto the stack to her right. The next one came off the stack on her left, and she started looking through this one page by page just like she had the four others before it.

Lying on her stomach on the living room floor of her own house, Darcy tapped her pencil against the yellow writing pad where she was taking careful notes. Not that there was much to take notes on so far. As soon as they'd gotten home she'd started pulling books from their shelves and from her closet and then she'd set herself up here, her feet kicked up in the air, ready to dive into this mystery.

So far, she hadn't found much of anything that was helpful.

Misty Hollow had been incorporated as a town back in 1846. Before that, the area had been named something else. Nothing she had here at the house told her much about the town before that. It had been settled, people came to live here, and then the name had been changed and the town had begun to grow up into what they knew Misty Hollow to be today.

And that was as far as she had gotten.

Twisting a strand of her hair she read through a couple of paragraphs on the page in front of her, then flipped to another section. Then another. Then she sighed and slammed the book shut. "This is useless."

"You can't find anything at all?" Jon asked from where he was sacked out on the couch. He'd flipped through the television channels for a few minutes after unsuccessfully trying to get her to eat something. He'd shut it off again after finding nothing that could hold his attention, but he'd stayed here in the living room with her just to keep her company.

"I can find bits and pieces of fun facts," she grumbled. "In ancient Jewish tradition, wandering spirits called Dybbuks could possess people. There was a whole exorcism ritual performed by the Baal Shem to cleanse the spirits out of people. Catholics have been performing exorcisms of demons since the 1500s and I've even got a few examples as recent as the 1970s."

"I didn't think Jews believed in the Devil and demons," Jon pointed out.

"They don't. It's the Catholics and other religions that believe possessions always involve demons."

"So…we're thinking this was a demon?"

She looked at him slantways with her eyebrows lowered and her lips pressed together.

"No. Of course not." He sat up straighter and spread his hands out helplessly. "Because that would be just plain crazy."

"I could do without the sarcasm, thank you." Darcy sighed, realizing she didn't have any reason to be mad at Jon. "Sorry. I'm just a little tense, I guess. I can't figure this out. Possessing spirits aren't always evil, no, but in this case I think there's a strong argument to say Nathaniel Williams isn't a friendly ghost."

"Definitely not getting that Casper vibe."

"No. Definitely not. Helen's in danger and we're all suspects in a murder even if no one but us knows it. I'm supposed to be the expert on all things ghosts and I can't figure this out!"

She slammed her fists into the carpeted floor and immediately wished she hadn't. The floor underneath was hard. The sides of her hands tingled painfully.

Ghost Story

Jon softened his tone. "Okay. I'm sorry, too. We're all stressed. Well, what about that thing you do to find out if people are guilty? Where you hold their hands and look for signs of blood on their hands?"

She thought it was cute how he tried to understand the things she could do. The technique he was talking about allowed her to see if people were feeling guilty about something they had done. She would be able to "see" spiritual, figurative blood on the hands of the guilty. It was a technique her Great Aunt Millie had laid out in a book she'd written on the subject of the paranormal. It had come in handy more than once, but it wouldn't help them here.

"That only works if the person actually feels guilty about something," she explained. She'd told him this same thing before, but she couldn't blame him for not understanding the finer points of her gift. She didn't even understand everything she could do yet. "If a person doesn't feel bad about killing someone, then there's no blood on their hands. In our case we were all passed out. If we don't even know what we did, or if we did anything at all, then there's no way for us to feel guilty about it."

He pursed his lips in thought. "I see what you mean. Do we really know if everyone was passed out? I mean, one of us had to still be awake, right? If one of us went off and killed someone then they had to be awake for it."

"If we were possessed, then whoever did it might not have been consciously aware of what they were doing, awake or not." She shrugged and rolled over onto her back. "Just like how Helen couldn't remember what she said to us because it was the ghost speaking through her. No memory of committing a sin, no guilt. I can try, I guess, but I don't know what good it would do."

An idea was nagging at her, but she couldn't quite think it through. Something either she or Jon had just said. She was getting an idea. Half an idea, anyway.

"None of us had real blood on our hands either," Jon pointed out, interrupting her thoughts. "Not the spiritual kind. The real stuff. There were a lot of cuts in that woman's abdomen. It was like a scene out of the Orient Express."

Murder on the Orient Express, Agatha Christie's novel about her super detective Hercule Poirot. Darcy so wished she had some of that mystery solving prowess to help her now. "I know. This one is different than our usual mysteries. Ghosts don't leave physical evidence behind."

"Actually..." Jon rubbed his fingers along his chin. "Come to think of it Helen did have blood on her hands, didn't she? Her arms, too. Remember?"

"Sure, but that was because she tore her fingernails on the table when she was in that trance." That was all it was. Darcy was sure of it.

"So we're back to the same question. Are we really sure we were all passed out? I mean, I know I was. I trust you when you say you were. Same with Grace and Aaron, but what about Helen and Andrew?"

Darcy admitted she had to at least consider the question. "I'm sure, if Helen says she was passed out, then she was. Andrew...I trust Andrew. I've known him for a while now and I've never known him to be dishonest. If he says he was passed out, then he was."

"Wait," Jon said. He held up his hand, looking down at the floor. She could see his eyes moving back and forth and she knew he was trying to remember something. She'd seen him use this technique any number of times when he was working on a case.

GHOST STORY

"Did he say...I mean, did Andrew actually say he had passed out? I don't remember him actually saying that. Do you?"

Caught off guard by that question, Darcy sat up, holding Jon's gaze as she thought back on the events in Helen's house. She tried to remember exactly what everyone had said. She had still been a little groggy, still dizzy and trying to get her bearings, but she remembered asking if everyone had passed out. She remembered what Jon had said, and Grace, and Aaron, and she remembered Helen nodding her head with that look of terror on her face...

But she didn't remember Andrew answering the question, one way or the other.

Plus, he had been almost confrontational with her about the whole possession thing. She had thought it was just because that was how some people reacted whenever she brought up the subject of ghosts, but could there have been a different reason?

A cold dread settled into the pit of her stomach. Maybe Andrew had stayed awake while all the rest of them had been rendered unconscious. Was it possible that he knew exactly what had happened, and who the murderer was?

Could he be the killer?

"Okay," she said, not liking where this was going. "I'll go back there tonight and ask both Helen and Andrew to sit for me to perform the ritual. If nothing else it should clear them both of having intentionally committing the murder."

"But not if they were possessed when they did it."

"Right. My aunt's technique only goes so far."

Her aunt's technique.

From her book.

That was what she had been trying to think of before. Her aunt's book was back at her store, along with her journal and a couple more books on the history of Misty Hollow. Those were the books she really needed.

"Jon, I need to go into town." She was already up and kissing him on the cheek. "I just remembered something at the bookstore that might help."

He caught her hand and pulled her back, kissing her lips firmly. "That's better. You want me to drive you in?"

"It's not that far, silly. I can walk."

She thought that would be the end of it, but he kept hold of her hand. His eyes were troubled.

"Jon," she said, "I'll be all right."

"I know. I know, it's just…what Helen said today. Well, what the ghost said through her, I guess. Any of us could be next. We're all in trouble. You most of all. I don't want to let you out of my sight."

She rolled her eyes, but really his concern made her warm inside. Besides, as much as it would kill her to say so, he was right. With her abilities so tuned to the other side, to the world of ghosts and things that went bump in the night, she would be more susceptible to any attacks that came from the spirit of Mister Nathaniel Williams.

"Okay," she told him. "You can come with me. It will be nice to have some company. Maybe we can talk more about choosing a date for our wedding."

"How about Halloween?" he joked with her as they went to the kitchen to get their jackets and the car keys. "That's just a few days away."

"Jon. I am not getting married on Halloween."

"Why not? Everyone loves Halloween. Instead of rice our guests can throw candy corn."

Ghost Story

"I hate candy corn." Darcy was smiling in spite of herself, and she was grateful that he could bring humor into even a crazy situation like this. "You and I will find the perfect date for our wedding and it will not, I repeat, not be Halloween."

The town usually did their Halloween celebration on the weekend before the thirty-first when the holiday fell during the week. That would have put it tonight, but the town council had decided to try trick or treating on the actual night this year to see how it went. All the kids in town would be going door to door in just a few days to get their free candy sugar rush, and she and Jon would not, under any circumstances, be getting married then.

Smudge came up to her at the door, rubbing between her legs. Her big black and white tomcat purred loudly, then looked up at her and meowed.

"I know, Smudge," she said, bending down to scratch between his ears. "We've been gone all day and now we're going out again. We won't be long. Just hold the fort for us here and let me know if any ghosts come knocking at the door."

When she said it, Smudge sneezed as if to say, "You're kidding, right?" Then he promptly dashed across the kitchen floor and into the living room.

"Some guard cat," Jon muttered. "Come on. Let's go. I'm freaked out by this one, I don't mind telling you. I want to find out what's going on, and fast, before someone else gets hurt."

Darcy nodded, agreeing with him completely. "Has anyone identified the victim yet? Wilson was working on that, wasn't he?"

"Back at the station, yes. That's what he gets for being the junior detective at the department." Jon held the door open for her and then locked it behind them again. "He hasn't called yet. I told him to let me know the minute they had anything."

"I thought I knew everyone in Misty Hollow. At least by sight."

"She didn't look familiar to any of us, Darcy. I don't know what that means."

Darcy didn't either.

⁓

The front window of the Sweet Read Bookstore had been replaced after debris from a terrible car accident had crashed through it. It had taken a week for the local hardware store to get the glass in and then another three days for them to install it. Darcy had used the opportunity to have the name of the store printed onto the window in gold, scripted letters. Below the name in a smaller size was Darcy's new slogan.

"The Mysterious is All Around Us."

She'd heard the phrase "isn't it mysterious?" so much in her life that she'd decided to adopt it as her unofficial motto. It had caught on, to an extent, and she'd had t-shirts and coffee mugs printed to sell in the shop in a wide range of colors. The mysterious is all around us.

Wasn't that the truth.

Several of the people in town had already complimented her on it. Apparently there were a lot of people other than herself who felt the strangeness in Misty Hollow, the odd sense that the paranormal was here and watching, waiting for an opening to slip into their lives.

Darcy glanced at her slogan now as Jon pulled up to the curb in front of the bookstore and really, really wished that there was just a bit less mystery in her life. Nancy Drew might have enjoyed getting caught up in enough mysteries to make a television series but Darcy wasn't a fictional heroine in some novel. The mysteries she got caught up in were real, and real people were getting hurt.

They got out of the car together and she took the key ring from her pocket to unlock the door. The store was never open on Sundays, but it was after seven o'clock now and normal business hours would have been over regardless. Flicking the lights on, she and Jon headed for the back office.

Paper pumpkins hung from the ceiling beside goofy cutouts of ghosts that looked more like kids wearing bed sheets than the real thing. Darcy didn't mind, though. It was decoration for Halloween. It wasn't meant to look real. It was meant to be something fun for the kids who came into the store.

She couldn't help but notice that several of the cutout ghosts had been turned upside down on their strings. Great Aunt Millie apparently wasn't as okay with the goofy looking ghosts as Darcy was.

"Looks like I have some redecorating to do tomorrow," Darcy grumped, knowing her aunt would hear her.

"Looks like," Jon agreed. "You really should fix that gouge in the floor, too."

"I know. It's on my list of things to do. Right after picking a date for our wedding."

He rolled his eyes at her and smiled.

The gouge was from the same piece of accident debris that had shattered her window. She'd meant to have the floorboards replaced by now, but it wasn't a priority. Besides, it gave her place character and was something for her customers to talk about.

Back past the rack of printed t-shirts and hooded sweatshirts, past the display of electronic readers, the door to the office stood open behind the checkout counter. A separate switch inside the door turned on the lights here, revealing a small rectangular space. Darcy's desk was crammed against the wall and two filing cabinets stood mostly unused and a shelf above the desk was filled with books that would never be for sale, ever.

Darcy reached up on her tiptoes to take down three books in particular. One was her aunt's journal, a small book with a black leather cover. Millie had spent a lot of time filling its pages with her personal observations of Misty Hollow. Darcy had been able to find help in her aunt's words time and time again and she was hoping there would be something in here to help her now.

The other two books were older volumes with pages that were starting to yellow and covers that were starting to fade. She and Jon had picked them up in a rare bookstore. They were books on the history of the area and the different towns and the people who had lived there. Misty Hollow was mentioned in there a few times. If they went back far enough, historically, then they might shed some light on who Nathaniel Williams was.

"I can't believe you haven't read through these already," Jon said to her. "Considering how much of a bibliophile you are."

"That's a pretty big word there, Mister Detective."

"Well, my girlfriend runs a bookstore. I've picked up a few things."

She smiled at him before sitting down to turn her attention to the books. The history books seemed the best way to start. Opening the first of the two in the set she hooked strands of her hair behind her ear and turned to the table of contents. Each chapter was labeled with the name of a story. Some of them she remembered, some she knew she hadn't read yet, and others she wasn't sure about.

The one near the end definitely had to do with Misty Hollow. She remembered that one. Turning to it, she skimmed through the narrative, knowing already it wouldn't be any help to her. It was about a railroad that had come through here at one point, only to be abandoned twenty years later in favor of the growing popularity of vehicle transport. Darcy knew where the tracks had been. Even today the ground was all gravel with the occasional rotting railroad tie sticking up out of the dirt. Interesting, but not useful.

Another short paragraph mentioned a fire that had destroyed the Town Hall on Main Street back in 1796. The building at the time, a wooden construction with timber beams and flooring, had burned to the ground and had to be reconstructed. It wouldn't be completely refinished until the turn of the century. Thereafter, several renovation projects had changed the look of the place again and again.

A few other stories turned out to be tales from Meadowood, or Parkerton, or Edwardsville, or some other nearby town. She found another one about Misty Hollow's original families, Helen's included, and she recognized the name of one of her ancestors as well in there, but there was no Williams family in the list.

Frustrated, she turned back to the table of contents.

"Jon, this is going to take a while. I'll need to read through the book my aunt published on paranormal techniques, too. Are you sure you want to stay with me?" She found one other story from Misty Hollow and turned to that page. "I promise I can take care of myself."

He stood behind her and kissed the top of her head. "I know you're a big girl, Darcy. But I care about you. You're going to have to accept me being protective sometimes."

"Like when psychotic ghosts kill people and leave them on the front lawn at our friends' houses?"

"Exactly."

There was a long pause as they both remembered what they had seen today. A dead woman, murdered by someone's hand. Worse was knowing that the hand involved belonged to one of them. Was it her? Darcy had wondered that more than once this afternoon. Jon was probably wondering if it was him, too. She didn't think she had done something that awful, but she had been blacked out and at the mercy of a crazed specter...

Darcy began to read the words on the pages in front of her. As she read, Jon kneaded the muscles along her shoulders and upper back with his fingers. It was too bad they weren't back at home doing this where she could really enjoy it...

The narrative she was reading caught her full attention. It was set in the late 1700s, a few decades before the area became Misty Hollow. Apparently, some sort of holiday had been declared in celebration of five straight years of bountiful harvest and prosperity. It kind of sounded like Thanksgiving, actually. The writer of the book had a very dry, textbook-like style that made what could have been an interesting story seem boring and dull, but Darcy trudged through the rest of it.

The celebration had been cut short when a riot broke out. A group of men armed with guns and knives and pitchforks had tried to seize the land by force, right there in broad daylight apparently. The leader of the group claimed that his family held the original title for the town and that the property had been stolen from him by the governor of the area, one Roderick Chauncy. People were killed during the chaos before it was finally stopped. A lot of people.

Five of the men responsible for the riot did penance for their deeds and were held in the stocks for a week. The leader of the group had a different fate. He was defiant to the end, and got himself hanged for his crimes. On the night before All Hallow's Evening.

Ghost Story

The night before Halloween.

In the Town Hall.

"I think I've found something," Darcy said, after she'd read the last paragraph two more times. "Look at this."

He read through the two pages of historical drama and then reached past her to tap his finger against the book. "This sounds like what our ghost was ranting about. How Misty Hollow was stolen from him. It doesn't name the guy who caused the riots, though."

"I noticed that, too. History has a way of forgetting certain things. This is a pretty obscure fact about the area history. We're lucky anything got recorded about it at all. I can't believe they hung people right in the Town Hall!"

"Hanging was a favorite form of capital punishment back in the day," Jon said. "Less bloody than beheadings, cheaper than a firing squad. The Town Hall would have served as the courtroom and the public meeting place as well. Kind of makes sense that if they were going to hang people then they would do it in the Town Hall."

"I suppose. It still seems a little gruesome."

"Yes, it does. So. How do we find out if Nathaniel Williams was the one who got hanged? Or if he's anyone for that matter. Do you think the ghost could have lied to us about who he is?"

Darcy shook her head. "Ghosts don't usually lie about who they are. Their identity is very important to them. That's not to say they might not have their own agenda. They just don't have all the reasons to lie that living people do. For the most part, it's impossible to get a ghost to give you a straight answer, let alone a lie."

"Well the dearly departed Nathaniel Williams certainly had a lot to say."

That was true, Darcy had to admit. "I think that's because he was possessing Helen. That was allowing him to speak through her. It's easier for a ghost to communicate when they have a host body. You know, a real mouth to talk with. That's what my Aunt Millie wrote out in her journal, anyway."

"Heh," Jon chuckled. "Dearly departed. Guess I can't call him that. Not sure it applies. Still, I understand what you're saying. So this is really the ghost of Nathaniel Williams, angry rampaging spirit. Now we just need to know what his problem is and we can…uh, what? Exorcise him? Open the door for him?"

"You know, I love how you try to understand what I do." She stroked his cheek and wished there was time for them, like there had been this morning. "Yes. Something like that. I've helped spirits cross over before. I've never performed an exorcism and I really didn't want to start now."

"What's the difference? Isn't that the same thing whether you call it crossing over or exorcism?"

"No, see, when I help spirits cross over, it's because they want to go. An exorcism involves forcing a dead person to leave the realm of the living. Emphasis on the force part. It's very serious stuff." Darcy had helped people in town "get rid" of ghosts from their houses before. Usually there was no ghost, but having Darcy say a few words in Latin and burn a few white candles made them feel better. "What we need to do is find out the ghost's backstory if we're going to be able to help him. Or help ourselves. I have the feeling we don't have much time to do it, either. Halloween is right around the corner."

"So?"

"So, if this person here is Nathaniel Williams, and he was hung on the night before Halloween, then that will be when he has the strongest connection to the world of the living. He felt pretty strong enough to me today. I don't want to see him when he gets stronger."

"I can't believe this," he said, his voice stressed. "I mean, I know ghosts are real, Darcy. I've seen you interact with them enough to know a fact when it hits me in the face. But this… This is something different. This is a ghost actually committing murder. I don't know if I'm ready for this."

"The ghost didn't commit murder," she corrected him. "Even the strongest of spirits can only move objects around a little. They couldn't stab a knife into someone over and over. That took a human's hand."

"A human possessed by a ghost. And didn't we just say how very strong this ghost was?"

"Psychic force. You were feeling it in your mind. We all were. That wasn't physical. Nathaniel Williams would have to be a ghost unlike anything I've ever seen to have done this himself."

"So we're back to one of us being the murderer."

Darcy didn't like it, but there it was. "Yup."

"One of us did it while we were possessed."

"Yup," she said again, shivering at the very thought.

Jon put his arms around her to lend her his warmth. "So where do we go now?" he asked. "Over to Helen's?"

"That's going to have to wait. I know someone who might be able to help us."

"Oh yeah? Who?"

"The town historian."

Chapter Four

They had taken over an hour at the bookstore looking through those books. It was getting close to nine o'clock, well past sunset, and the stars overhead cast faint silvery light down on the Earth. It shimmered on ethereal tendrils of mist that clung possessively to the edges of buildings and to the trunks of trees planted along the sidewalks.

"Is this the place?" Jon asked her. The house was a gray three story place with tall windows that were probably the originals from when the place was first built. An apple tree spread its branches in the front yard, the leaves turning shades of reds and yellows for autumn. Jon parked in the driveway and craned his neck to look up at the house through the windshield. Whistling, he said, "Wow. I'd hate to have to be the one to paint this place."

"Benson LaCroix is in his eighties, Jon. I doubt he paints his own house anymore."

"Still. Houses this big are a lot of work. Maybe he should have sold it to that cellphone company that wanted to put up a tower here. Might have been easier for him."

Darcy sort of agreed with him, but still. "It's his home. His family grew up here, if I remember correctly, just like my house belonged to Aunt Millie before me, and to her mother before that. Some people get attached to places like that."

Ghost Story

"Yeah, I can understand how that could happen. Still. A lot of work."

She leaned over and kissed his cheek. "Tell you what. I promise that when you're in your eighties I'll hire someone to take care of our house. Okay?"

He squeezed her hand, then kissed the knuckles of her fingers. "Deal. Come on. Let's go see what the town historian can tell us."

Their footsteps echoed on the long porch. The air was chilly, and Darcy tucked her arms around herself as Jon knocked on the heavy wooden door. She really wished that she had something more than her light jacket with her. Note to self, she thought. The next time she went investigating a mystery, she was going to dress in layers.

There were still lights on inside Benson's home. Darcy had been worried he would be in bed already. She shouldn't have worried, because after a few seconds she heard him inside. "Hold on, now, hold on," he called to them. "Just let me get my slippers."

Jon's cell phone rang at the same time that Benson opened the door. Excusing himself, he stepped back off the porch and over to the car. Darcy knew from the way he answered that it was the police department, and she wondered if they had maybe identified the woman who had been lying dead on Helen's lawn. Benson was standing in front of her, however, and she didn't have time to ask about the call.

"Well, hey there Darcy Sweet," Benson said to her. He folded his purple bathrobe tighter over his pajamas and gave her a bright smile. His eyes were magnified behind the lenses of his glasses. "What brings you over to my home so late at night?"

Benson was a nice old man who was still as sharp as a tack. Even if his dark ebony skin had faded a little with age and his curly hair had turned white, he would never be considered feeble. He'd been here in Misty Hollow longer than Darcy could remember and it seemed fitting that he was in charge of the museum and the historical documents for the town.

"I'm sorry to bother you so late, Benson," Darcy said by way of greeting. "I was wondering if you might have some time for me to pick your brain?"

"Might not be much there to pick," he joked, with a little laugh, "but anything I can do to help you, I'm always here. You know that. Come on in."

She followed him in, glancing over her shoulder at Jon. He was intent on the phone call and didn't notice her.

Inside, Benson brought them to the living room and motioned for her to sit on a plush gray couch. He sat opposite her in a recliner that looked just as comfortable, his checkered pajama bottoms hanging loosely as he crossed his legs. Darcy had been in his home before and she liked how cozy it seemed, with deep brown carpeting and walls painted a warm forest green. She also appreciated how nearly every room had a bookshelf or two, full of everything from fiction novels to technical manuals. More than a few of those had been purchased from her own shop.

"Now then," Benson said to her, settling his glasses on his nose and then steepling his fingers at his chest. "What can I do for the famous Darcy Sweet?"

"Famous?" she repeated, a bemused expression on her face. "What makes you say that?"

"Don't be so modest! That whole affair last month with the car accident on Main Street? That got picked up by the national news, you know. You're all but a household name nowadays."

Darcy shifted uncomfortably on the couch. She knew that the accident and the investigation surrounding it had made headlines. There had even been a few phone calls to her home asking for an interview. She was used to people in Misty Hollow jokingly asking for her autograph, but national news? She didn't know how she felt about that.

"Um. Well, something else has happened and I need your help. No one knows the history of Misty Hollow better than you."

He nodded, pride shining in his eyes. "That's true. Don't no one know half the things I do. Did you know there used to be a group of Shakers settled here? That was quite the scandal back then, let me tell you."

"That's interesting," Darcy said, not meaning to cut him off but wanting to keep the conversation on topic. Jon would come back any minute, probably with the name of their victim, and they couldn't afford to get caught up in long historical anecdotes. "Benson, if I asked you about a man named Nathaniel Williams who used to live here in Misty Hollow, would you be able to tell me anything about him?"

Benson froze where he sat, his smile rigid, his hands perfectly still. Darcy wasn't even really sure he was breathing until he blinked and licked his lips. "Nathaniel Williams. Now, why would you want to go and ask about him?"

"Well," Darcy said, thinking quickly, "his name came up in connection with the Town Hall today and I can't seem to find anything about him anywhere so I was hoping that you knew something."

He stared at her, and Darcy could feel his reluctance to talk. He swallowed, and nodded his head, and got up from his chair. He looked different as he did. Older, Darcy thought. His arms shook as he pushed himself up and his feet shuffled on the carpet. "On second thought it is kind of late, Darcy. Tell you what.

Why don't we save this question for some other time. Tomorrow, maybe? Yes. Tomorrow. That'd be good."

Darcy didn't understand. "Benson, I kind of need to know about this now. The longer I wait, the worse things are going to be…"

She realized she'd said too much, more than she had intended to, and she tried to stop herself but it was too late. She could see that Benson had already figured out this was much more than just a casual question on her part.

"Something bad done happened, didn't it?" he asked her.

She could have lied. She didn't, even though it would have made things easier. "Yes, Benson. Something bad happened. A woman has been murdered. You know what I can do. What my abilities allow me to do. I've talked to you about it before. I think the ghost of Nathaniel Williams is involved in the killing, and I think there's going to be more of it, if I don't figure this out."

Not to mention that the ghost had apparently used one of them to kill that woman. That part was probably best left unsaid, Darcy thought. At least for now.

"Yes," the older man mumbled. "Sooner. Sooner rather than later."

"I'm sorry, what?" Darcy asked.

He brought his eyes back up to focus on her and smiled almost apologetically. "Darcy Sweet, you just have this magnetism about you, now don't you? You attract trouble like honey attracts flies."

Darcy figured that she'd been compared to worse things than honey. He was right, though. Trouble seemed to find her here in this quiet little community.

He took in a deep breath and then sighed it out heavily. "Well, come on then. Let's go on down to my study."

Ghost Story

Benson's house might be three stories high but it wasn't very big in terms of floor space. The living room fed right into the kitchen and dining room, and then off that was a smaller room that was built floor to ceiling with shelves stuffed with books. A small desk of dark wood sat in the very center of the room. Papers and more books filled up the desktop. Benson walked around to the chair behind the desk and sat down.

"Uh, I had another chair in here," he said, looking around at everything. "Oh, there it is. Over there in the corner under the collected works of Shakespeare. Just put them books down on the floor and scoot that chair on over here, will you?"

Two thick tomes, both with soft brown covers featuring a picture of the Bard holding a rolled piece of parchment, were on the seat of a folding metal chair. Darcy moved them carefully to the floor like he had asked her to, then carried the flimsy chair over. Benson had already taken a book off one of the shelves behind him and opened it up on top of everything else on the desk.

"Misty Hollow's got a long and sordid past," he started. "Most folks don't know that. Way back when, this whole area wasn't nothing but trees and rocks and a few wooden shacks. Group of ten people came here to scratch out a living. Wasn't no religious community like the Quakers or the Adventists. Just a group of friends who wanted to make money off owning the land and selling it to newcomers. Kind of a get rich quick scheme. That's where Misty Hollow came from. Wasn't even called that back then. Had a different name."

The chair was just as uncomfortable as it had looked as Darcy sat down in it. She listened to Benson talk, picturing the events of the town's creation as Benson told them. It was the same story she'd read earlier, but he was filling in the bare facts with real description and making it possible for Darcy to imagine being there. "What did the town used to be called?"

"Had high hopes for the place, those original settlers. Called it New Heaven." He paused, tapping a finger against the page in front of him. "Turned out to be more like New Hell. See, these folks who bought the land here called themselves friends but there was always bad blood between them. Two in particular. Those two were the leaders of that little group, but they sure weren't friends. Roderick Chauncy was one of them. Other was Nathaniel Williams."

Darcy startled as something sleek and heavy jumped up from the floor, landing softly in her lap. Benson's pretty gray cat with the white tipped ears looked up at Darcy with a little mewl, then settled into a curled up ball and let Darcy rub her fur. "For Pete's sake, Twistypaws," Darcy greeted the feline. She waited for her heart to settle back down from where it had leapt into her throat. "How about next time you wait for the ghost story to be over before you pounce on me like that, okay?"

Chuckling, Benson continued his tale. "Now. This feud of theirs continued for a few years. Lots happened in them early years, but nothing that will interest you right now. The wilderness started becoming a town. More people came in. Fast forward to the year 1795, and you'll see an all-out war between Williams and Chauncy over who actually owns the land. Turned into a mini civil war, from everything I can piece together. They tried to kill each other. Both them had their supporters, with everything from muskets to pitchforks to bare hands and teeth. Ended up with a handful of people dead before Nathaniel Williams and his people finally got arrested by Misty Hollow's first ever lawman."

He looked at her with a raised eyebrow, obviously waiting for her to ask something.

"Wait. You don't mean…?" Darcy knew her family had come from some of the first settlers in the area. One of her cousins had traced their roots back to England, proudly displaying her lineage map at a family get together. From overseas, the family had migrated here, to this very spot. But could it be? "Who was the lawman?"

"Fellow by the name of Whitmarsh Grace. He got himself elected by the group living here to put an end to the feud. That's exactly what he did. Seems to me your mother named your sister after that part of the family."

Actually, that wasn't the reason at all. Darcy's mom had been so happy at the birth of her first baby that she had declared it a miracle, and so her older sister had been given the name Grace. Now that Benson mentioned it, though, maybe there had been more to it. Maybe the old family name had influenced her mom more than she had realized.

So her great, great, great, great, and so on ancestor had been responsible for arresting Nathaniel Williams. "What did he do?" she asked. "I mean, to arrest those people?"

Benson turned a page. There was a full color reprint of a painting, an artist's rendering of a man hanging from thick rafters inside a building somewhere while people looked on with grim faces. His dark fingers slid across the picture like he was reading the scene by touch alone. "Didn't exactly arrest them. More like beat them all to within an inch of their lives. He got him a few deputies who liked to do their talking with their fists and rounded everyone up. There was six of them in Williams' group. Every single one of them faced hanging for the murders they'd done. Five of them repented and placed the blame at Williams' feet. Said it was all his idea. Those five got sent to the stocks for a week, starving out in the weather, locked in place, while people spit at them and threw garbage in their faces."

Without looking, his finger settled over Nathaniel Williams. Right where his heart would be in the painting.

"Williams here, he got himself hung for the crime. With his dying breath, he cursed Roderick Chauncy. Cursed the town. Cursed everyone. Said he would rise up from his grave and kill everyone."

"The story I read said he was killed for being a witch."

Benson shook his head. "Nope. Wasn't no witch. Wasn't no Pilgrim either, but that don't stop people from calling him that. He was just a jealous, money hungry man angry at the whole wide world."

Darcy looked at the painting of the man who would come to be known as the Pilgrim Ghost, hanging from a rope as punishment for his sins. She studied his face. It was the angry visage of a man who had been wronged, a man who hated everyone, and everything. The rest of the picture was just as vivid, from the faces of the gawkers to the timbers of the Town Hall to the intricate designs carved into the beam the hangman's noose was suspended from. Even the grandfather clock standing in the corner was rendered in perfect detail. The hands showed Darcy the time of the hanging. Eleven fifty-nine. Through the windows she saw the black sky of night.

It was one minute before midnight.

The exact time that the clock on the Town Hall was stuck at.

The door to the study burst open and Darcy jumped up from her chair, unseating Twistypaws. The poor cat streaked out of the room between Jon's legs, like a streak of furry lightning.

"Sorry," Jon said to them. "I didn't mean to let the door bang like that. Hi, Benson. Do you mind if I borrow Darcy for a moment?"

"Sure, sure. Kind of the end of my tale, anyway."

GHOST STORY

He went to stand up, but Darcy had one more question.

"Did Williams ever make good on his threat?" Coming from anyone else that would have seemed a bizarre thing to ask. Ghosts couldn't curse people. They couldn't rise up from the grave and exact revenge.

Except in Darcy's world, they could. And did.

Benson settled back into his seat, with a sad nod of his head. "In 1796, year after Williams was hung, the Town Hall burnt down. With Roderick Chauncy in it. Five decades later, the main support beam in the new Town Hall cracked and came crashing down on the head of Whitmarsh Grace's grandson. Boy died where he stood. Other things have happened here in Misty Hollow, if you haven't noticed. Some of it is just normal small town stuff. But the rest of it? No, sir. Can't be this much evil in one town less it has a source."

He didn't say what that source was, but the implication of his words was clear.

"Darcy, I need to talk to you," Jon whispered. "Now."

"Okay. Benson, thank you," she said. The old man only nodded, staring down at the picture of the hanging Nathaniel Williams. He was lost in thoughts too dark to share, perhaps, or worrying about the ones he had already shared.

They left him there in his study, and Jon ushered them out of the house as quickly as he could. Twistypaws watched them with quiet cat reserve, looking like she had already forgotten about the fright Darcy had given her. Although the way her tail twitched Darcy wasn't so sure.

Out in the driveway, at the car, Jon huddled close to Darcy and held his voice pitched low. "They identified the woman."

"Really? Who was she?" Darcy was still processing what Benson had told her inside. She wanted to know who the victim was and how she could possibly fit into the nightmarish history that Misty Hollow had come from.

"Her name was Bonnie Verhault. She was a real estate agent."

"So, nobody from Misty Hollow."

"No. That's why none of us recognized her. We didn't know her. But guess what she was doing in town?"

"Jon, how could I know…" Real estate agent, Darcy thought. What did real estate agents do? "She was here to buy property? Here in Misty Hollow."

"You got it. Specifically she was here looking to buy land out on Coldspring Road next to where the new Dollar Store complex is going in." He smiled grimly, like he'd swallowed something sour. "Wilson did some digging, looking to see who owned the land out there, to see if maybe whoever owned it would have a grudge against her for buying it. Guess what name the property is listed under?"

Darcy felt a chill go up her spine. "Williams. It's the Williams family land."

"You got it. It's belonged to their family since back in the 1700s. None of them still live in Misty Hollow, but they still hold the deed in absentia."

Things were starting to come together, but Darcy didn't like the way it was shaping up. Nathaniel Williams was a murderous spirit, intent on revenge and holding onto what he thought was his, even from the grave.

How was she supposed to stop him?

Chapter Five

Jon drove straight to the police station. He wanted to help Wilson with the case, both to pitch in for the department and to find out if they had learned anything more about Bonnie Verhault.

He had been very insistent that Darcy stay with him. As much as she wanted to do exactly that, she needed to get home. She wanted to call and check on Grace and Aaron, not to mention Helen and Andrew. Then there was Smudge to take care of. Well, he could take care of himself, pretty much, but she hated leaving him alone for so long. They were best friends, after all.

Jon had argued with her, but in the end she won out. With an exasperated sigh he drove her to their house, insisting that she call him if anything at all happened. She agreed, kissing his forehead to seal the promise.

Mostly, she wanted to get home to consult with her books and see what would be involved in exorcising a two hundred year old ghost from the town. No doubt there would be a lot involved in it. Whenever she did a communication, calling on the ghost of someone who had passed on, it took something out of her. An outpouring of her personal energy. A piece of her soul, kind of. What would a full on exorcism cost her?

The house was quiet when she got back. It was close to eleven o'clock now, and the day had been exhausting. Especially for one that had started out so lazily with just her and Jon hanging out together. Darcy sighed as she poured a cup of tea for herself, standing in the kitchen. When she and Jon got married they would have to honeymoon far, far away from Misty Hollow if they expected to have any time at all for just the two of them. Australia seemed nice. Maybe they could go there.

The phone calls themselves had taken over an hour. Grace was very matter of fact in asking questions and getting information, but then had choked up a little when she talked about how scared she had been for baby Addison. Darcy remembered the little voice in the back of her mind while Nathaniel Williams' ghost had railed at them, and had no problem admitting that she was worried for Addison, too. The sisters promised to watch out for the newborn child, no matter what.

The conversation with Helen had taken a lot longer. She was an emotional wreck, terrified by what had happened and what might happen and unsure what to do about either. As the town's mayor, she needed to make sure the citizens of Misty Hollow were safe. She had a certain image to uphold for the community, as well, and dead bodies showing up on her lawn didn't exactly help her with that. Not that her image was anything more than a minor concern.

Her real concern, was who had killed Bonnie Verhault.

That was Darcy's concern, too.

After promising to call Helen the minute she knew anything else, Darcy had finally been able to relax a bit. After locking both doors and all the windows. She'd had her experiences with ghosts trying to break into the house before, and with human intruders as well. She had told Jon she was a big girl, and that was true, but she wasn't stupid.

Ghost Story

After changing out her jeans and her shirt for a pair of pink fleece pajamas, Darcy took her tea to the couch and curled up on the one end, with her feet tucked up underneath her.

Smudge came around the corner of the couch and jumped up next to her. She reached down to stroke the top of his head between his ears. "Hey there," she said to him. "Guess what? I saw Twistypaws today."

He blinked up at her, nuzzling his face against her fingers, as if to say, "Sure. I know."

Darcy smiled at him. "Of course you know. You always know."

The tea had a warming, soothing effect on her, just like her tomcat's comfortable presence did. Before long, she felt herself drifting off to sleep. It was late. She should be researching in her books, but sleep sounded so good right now. Jon would be home soon, she hoped, but he had his own key to get in. Right now, she had just a few moments to herself, and she wanted to spend them catching as much of a nap as she could.

"Don't sleep too long. You've got a lot to do."

She looked down next to her, where the familiar voice had come from. Smudge smiled up at her with his tail flicking gently against the couch. "Sorry," he said to her. "I know you just want to sleep."

"I really do, Smudge," she said, her voice heavy and drowsy. "I'm really tired."

He rubbed his head against the side of her leg. "I know. You should be like me. Sleep during the day. That way you can stay up at night."

"That's fine for you. I've got things to do during the day."

"So do I," he agreed. "Sleeping is one of them."

Darcy scratched his ears again. "I'm glad you're always here for me, Smudge. I don't mind telling you, I'm scared this time."

"You deal with ghosts all the time," Smudge reminded her.

"Not like this. This ghost…he's already killed once. He's going to kill again if I don't stop him."

"Are you sure about that?"

That was an odd question, she thought to herself. "Of course I'm sure. Smudge, I saw the body."

"What did you see?" he asked her, regarding her in that way that cats did so well whenever they knew something you didn't.

"It's a fair question, Darcy," said a kindly voice. A woman's voice.

She sat in the chair opposite the couch, across from Darcy, her long dark dress matched with a pearl necklace this time. Her floppy hat with its wide brim sat at an angle on her head, her white hair tucked neatly inside. Aunt Millie had taken to wearing that hat all the time now. Darcy kind of thought it suited her.

"You did tell me there would be worse coming," Darcy said to her.

Picking up her own cup of tea, Millie winked. "Sweetheart, did you think I'd leave you all alone to face this? I'm always here when you need me. You know that."

Darcy couldn't help but smile. She wasn't at all surprised to see her dead aunt coming to visit. After all, this was a dream.

"I know I can always ask you for help, Millie," Darcy told her, honestly grateful that she was here now. "I just don't understand why you stay around. The other side must be calling to you. You lived a good life. You deserve your rest now."

"Oh, tish tosh," Millie tsked. "I have a few more things to check on. Maybe a skeleton or two in my own closet to work out. Nobody is perfect, you know."

Ghost Story

Darcy had trouble believing that her Great Aunt had any dark issues still holding her to this mortal coil. There was a question here, about why Millie's spirit had yet to cross over. A mystery to be solved. Darcy knew she was the only one who could do it.

"Now, you let that be," Millie scolded her. "We're not worrying about me. Not when there's something worse to worry ourselves over."

"She's always been like that," Smudge said with a yawn, turning over onto his back and stretching. "Darcy thinks about everyone else's needs first. It's just one of the many reasons why I love her."

"Aw," Darcy said. "I love you too, Smudge."

"Darcy, I'm serious," Millie continued. "You've seen what Nathaniel Williams can do. You've got yourself one dead woman to worry about already. There might be more, if you don't put a stop to him."

"I know, Aunt Millie. It's more complicated than that, though. One of us killed that woman. I need to figure out which one. But if I do, then whoever it was will be facing a murder charge. I've got no way to defend my friends from this, but I still need to figure it out. I have to."

"Do you?" Millie seemed surprised by that idea. Then, with a shrug, she set her cup of tea down on the coffee table between them, next to Darcy's. "I suppose. Finding out who killed that poor woman won't necessarily help you stop Nathaniel Williams."

"I know he has to be stopped. I want to stop him. No. I need to stop him." Darcy heard the conviction in her voice, felt the heat in her face. She had rarely been this sure about anything in her life. "I don't know how, is the thing. I'm not an exorcist."

"Oh, neither was I," Millie said with a smile. "But I did my fair share. There's a method, and there's a way. The method is in a book. Spelled out for you all nice and neat. It's right up there, sweetheart."

She pointed up at the wall behind the couch. Darcy turned to find Smudge up on the shelf Millie was indicating, pulling a book with a red cover out with his teeth. "Thif if it," he said around a mouthful of book spine.

"Hey, don't you ruin my books!" Darcy scolded him. She knew which book Millie meant. She'd read through it last night in her search for clues about Nathaniel Williams' ghost. Exorcism 101, basically. "Okay, Millie, that's the method. You said there was a method, and a way. If that's the method then what's the way?"

Her Great Aunt reached out and took her hands, holding them in her own, studying them closely. "Oh, my. What pretty rings you have."

Darcy rolled her eyes. "You've seen my rings before, Millie. I wear them all the time in the shop. One of them was yours, remember?"

The world around her, the dream world, violently rocked sideways as lines blurred across her vision like something was trying to tear it apart.

It hurt. A lot.

"Millie," Darcy said in alarm, "what was that?"

"Hm. I was afraid he'd find you here. I just thought we'd have more time. I always wish there was more time."

She shook her head sadly and reached for her tea cup again.

The table bounced up on two legs and then thumped back down to the floor, knocking both cups off with enough force to shatter them, tea spilling out across the rug. Darcy gripped the arm of the couch, holding on tightly against a sudden invisible force trying to pull her away.

"Millie!" she screamed.

"It's right where it belongs, you know," was her aunt's calm reply. "It's where it's always been, right where it belongs. It's right—"

The world turned upside down and Darcy was looking at the floor above her and the ceiling beneath her as she fell upward. The dream was being shredded around her. Some dark force that she couldn't see had ahold of her and would not let go.

She was being attacked.

"It's right where it belongs," Millie said again, as her image smeared and drifted away into nothing. "It's where it's always been. It's right where it belongs."

Then Darcy woke up.

⁓

She was on the floor, a warm, dark liquid seeping out under her. A dark form hovered over her, shadows that might have been someone or no one or nothing at all. Darcy could feel the pain of the beating she had just taken, the attack that had woken her up from her sleep. Everywhere hurt. Was she bleeding? She reached up with her hands to ward off her attacker.

His hands grabbed hers. He held her down, held her in place, and shouted at her.

Darcy screamed.

"Hold on!" he said. A very strange thing for an attacker to say. "Calm down. Darcy, calm down. It's me."

Her eyes finally managed to come back into focus and she forced herself to concentrate on the face that hovered so close to hers, on the man who was holding her down on her own living room floor.

Jon. It was Jon.

Sobbing, breaking down into hot tears, Darcy allowed him to scoop her up into his arms and hold her. "Ow," she managed, sucking in a breath between her tears. "Jon. Careful, it hurts."

"What happened?" he asked her, loosening his grip but not letting go. "I came in the house and I found you here on the floor. What happened?"

She remembered feeling the warm wetness under her and in a panic she reached up to feel the back of her head, her neck, her shoulders…there. Her fingers came away wet and she brought them up in front of her face and for a moment she was sure it was blood until she smelled the bittersweet aroma and realized she had landed in the spilled tea from where it had been knocked off the coffee table. She looked down now and saw the broken teacups.

Two cups. Hers…and Aunt Millie's.

"I was attacked," Darcy told Jon. "Somebody…somebody broke into the house and they were…hitting…beating me…" She couldn't remember what had happened, now that she was trying to. There had been the very vivid dream with her and Smudge and Millie and then there had just been this topsy-turvy feeling of being dragged off the couch and thrown around and now everything hurt.

Jon was looking at her very intently. "Darcy. There's no one else in the house but us. The door was still locked when I got here."

"But Jon, it was real. It happened."

"Okay, okay. I believe you." His tone didn't sound all that convinced. "But if you were attacked, where is the guy? How could he get by me? Do you think he's still in the house?"

Darcy wasn't thinking that at all. She was thinking about possessing spirits and how the people who were possessed rarely remembered what the ghost had done through them. She was thinking how she had woken up being beaten and then seen Jon standing directly over her.

No. Oh, God no.

"Jon," she said slowly. "Can you stand over there? For just a minute. Please?"

His brows knitted. "What's wrong?"

"Just go over there. On the other side of the living room." She pushed at him, gently but firmly, and he let her go. She stepped back, slowly, wishing she wasn't thinking what she was thinking.

One of the people at the party had been possessed and forced to kill a woman. Now Jon was here, right here, while she was being beaten. It couldn't be him. It couldn't.

The pain in her arms and legs and all the rest of her said otherwise.

"Jon, please don't panic. I need to check your spirit."

"You need to…what?"

"Your aura, Jon. You need to let me see if Williams is still in you."

His eyes practically bugged out of his head. "Darcy don't be stupid. I'm fine. I didn't do anything."

"You wouldn't remember if you did. Just stand there. Right there, no closer. Please, Jon? Just for a few seconds."

While he was trying to stutter an argument Darcy raised her hands towards him and closed her eyes and reached out with her own spirit, the energies of her soul, and felt for his. She found it easily, the familiar warmth of his character that she had experienced so often, when he would hug her in the morning or walk with her at night or listen to her talk about her day. It was him. Purely him, and no one else.

"He's gone Jon. He's not in you anymore."

"Darcy, he was never in me! I was not possessed. It wasn't me."

She ran to him and threw herself in his arms. They held each other tightly, and she didn't bother arguing with him. She was hurting. Someone had attacked her, and there was no one else here but Jon.

And if Nathaniel Williams had possessed Jon just now to do this to her, then the prime suspect in the murder of Bonnie Verhault had just become her own fiancé.

Chapter Six

"You don't think you're being just a little ridiculous?"

"No," Darcy said to him honestly. "I don't."

She was still sore all over, but it was only a dull throbbing now and a twinge that tweaked her back whenever she reached up above her head.

"Ow."

Like that.

The book that Millie and Smudge had shown her in the dream was heavier than she remembered it. Sitting at the kitchen table, she opened it up to read. The red cover was soft in her hand like old leather got sometimes. It was too bad, in her opinion, that all books weren't still bound in leather like this. Aside from how hard that would be on the cow population, she enjoyed the heft and feel of a book like this. Then again, her bookstore was only making money now because of how she was able to sell e-books.

Technology was wonderful, but it sure made life confusing.

"What's in that book?" Jon asked.

"The instructions to do the exorcism." At least, she hoped that's what was there.

"Hmm."

His tone was still offended. No matter what she said or how she explained it he refused to believe he had been possessed by a ghost. She didn't blame him for the attack. If anything, she figured she hadn't been hurt worse than she was exactly because it was Jon doing the…what was done to her. He probably had resisted whatever Nathaniel Williams had made him do because of how much he loved her.

"Jon, just trust me, okay? I know what I'm doing."

Looking over at the windows, then back at her, he raised one eyebrow.

"It works!" she protested.

"I'm sure. Listen, putting salt across the windowsills is one thing, but I'm going to be tracking it through the house for a week from where you laid it in front of the doors."

There were certain rules that remained constant when dealing with ghosts. They were rarely easy to understand even when they managed to contact the living. They could not be seen by most people. They were annoyingly evasive. They missed their loved ones. Things like that.

Then there were a few truly weird facts about ghosts. Like they could not cross a line of salt.

Maybe one day Darcy would have the chance to write a book on the science of spiritual visitations. They were as immutable as the laws of physics, really. People had just as much use for knowing how to protect their home from ghosts as they did for knowing the periodic table of elements, and there were a ton of textbooks about the elements. So why not one on ghosts?

There had been two round containers of household salt up in the cabinets. Darcy had used everything in both of them to lace the windows and the doors, too. No way was she going to let the Pilgrim Ghost back in here for round two.

Ghost Story

She looked over at Jon. Then looked away quickly.

"Stop that," he said, pointing at her. "I saw that."

"I'm sorry," she mumbled. She couldn't help it, though. The thought that someone so close to her could have been taken over so easily scared her to death. What would have happened if she hadn't woken up when she did? Or, worse, if it had been someone besides Jon who had been available for the possessing?

"Darcy, I did not attack you. I came into the house and found you on the floor."

She didn't argue with him. There was no reason to debate it again with him. She'd spent nearly a half an hour trying to explain that when people were possessed by ghosts they didn't always remember what the ghost did while in their body. She'd checked him over, felt for another spirit being overlaid on his, and there wasn't any. Nathaniel Williams had left him alone. For now.

She wasn't afraid of Jon, necessarily. He hadn't done anything to her. It might have been his hands that did the attacking, but it had not been his mind, his spirit. It hadn't been him.

The thought of him killing Bonnie Verhault in that same sort of state, with his hands stabbing her over and over while his mind went on hiatus, was even more disturbing to her. Neither of them had brought that up. What would they do if physical trace evidence linked Jon to that crime? The Devil made me do it had gone out of style as a defense decades ago.

There was nothing they could say that would make that killing all right. For the police, or for Jon either. Darcy knew what kind of man he was. Knowing that he had killed a woman, whether or not he was possessed when he did it, would tear him apart.

"Look," she said instead, "we've got the ghost locked out of here for right now. Let's just make use of our time and find out what we need to stop him for good."

"Fine by me," he grumped. "So this is an Exorcism 101 textbook?"

"Something like that," she agreed, managing a wisp of a smile at Jon's wry sense of humor. No matter what, he would always be Jon to her.

In her dream, Great Aunt Millie had told her that there was a method and a way to do the exorcism. Two separate things. The method would be spelled out in the book. Forms, conjurings to recite, that sort of thing. All of that could be spelled out in black and white. The way to do the exorcism was different. Hopefully, the book would point her toward that as well.

When Darcy did a communication, it was a calling for a particular ghost to come to her. She provided a path for them to connect with her for a little while. By doing so, a ghost could find its way back to the realm of the living to speak to her. An exorcism was the exact opposite. The exorcism would provide a way for a ghost to leave the Earth, for good. It was like pushing an unwanted houseguest out of a door. The exorcism opened the door. That was the method. But she also would need something to create the way to the door and out the other side.

A method, and a way.

Starting at the first page of the book, Darcy smelled the pleasant scent of old paper, felt the smooth texture of the pages beneath her fingers. She loved books. It was comforting to have something this solid and real in her hands as she searched for the answers they needed.

Page by page, she read through the carefully written text of the book. Searching from the front to the back, she soon got to the last page. Then she frowned, flipped the page back and forward again, wondering if she had missed something.

There was nothing there.

Ghost Story

Darcy blinked. That couldn't be right. Why would Millie and Smudge point her towards a book that had nothing to do with the problem at hand? She thought back to her dream, remembering every detail that she could. No. This was definitely the book that Millie had pointed to. The one Smudge had tried to take off the shelf in his teeth.

Flipping back to page one, she read through it again. She smelled the pleasant scent of old paper, felt the smooth texture of the pages beneath her fingers as she turned them one after the other, reading through the carefully printed words of each chapter. There was a lot of information in this book. A lot of interesting facts about ghosts and the world of the hereafter.

Nothing on exorcisms.

"What is it?" Jon asked.

"It's not here," Darcy said, scrunching her eyebrows, not able to believe what she was seeing. "There's nothing in this book on exorcisms at all, Jon."

"Are you sure?" He came to stand behind her, leaning down over her shoulder. "Because I was sure I saw…right here. What's this?"

Darcy looked down to where his finger pointed at a title in bold, illuminated letters. She sighed patiently and turned to look up at him. "That isn't what we're looking for. We need to learn about exorcisms. How is this going to help?"

He stared at her blankly. "Because that's what it says."

She had been about to argue with him more but the words died on her lips. What was he talking about? Turning back to the book, she ran her fingers over the title he had indicated, smelling the pleasant scent of old paper, feeling the smooth texture of the page as she started to rip it out of the book.

"Darcy!" he shouted, grabbing her hands. "Darcy stop it! What are you doing?"

She struggled against him, making the neat tear she had started along the inside edge of the page cut away in a jagged line across the middle of the paper. She gasped and pulled her hands away from the book as fast as she could, shocked at what she had done.

"Jon…I don't understand." She didn't, either. Had she really done that? What was she thinking? "Look, I'm sorry. I guess I'm just frustrated because I can't find what I need. We have to do something about Nathaniel Williams now, before he gets someone else hurt."

Jon looked like he was ready to pounce on her again if he needed to, but he pointed back down at the page of the book she had nearly ruined. "Darcy. Look at what it says right there. Tell me what you see."

They didn't have time for games like this, and she was furious that he was going on about what simply wasn't there, but she did as he asked anyway, figuring it would be the quickest way to get back to actually finding answers to this mystery. Staring down at the title on the page she read the words, then turned back to him.

And forgot what she had just read.

Jon's eyes showed her that he knew what had just happened to her. She saw concern there, but also a little fear. This was silly. It simply didn't say anything important. Turning in her chair again she read the title one more time.

Only, it was gone again as soon as she read it.

Concentrating, focusing harder, she saw the letters squiggle on the page and blur and twist until she clenched her jaw and narrowed her eyes and made them stay in place so she could read them.

Ghost Story

"The Art of the Exorcism Method." That was what they said. The exact thing her aunt had wanted her to find.

"How…?" she breathed, not understanding what was happening. She reached out with trembling fingers as she quickly read through the page, the words presenting themselves plainly where they had escaped her attention before. It was all here. The knowledge she needed, wrapped up with the pleasant scent of old paper and the smooth feel of the page between her fingers as she pulled it away from the spine completely and began tearing it into tiny pieces.

"Darcy, stop!" Jon had her by her wrists but she had already torn the page in two. He grabbed the one half from her and stuffed it into his back pocket but that left her hands free to tear the other half into pieces too tiny to ever be put back together again.

"Why?" he asked her. "Darcy, look at what you're doing!"

Her fingers were still trying to tear the pieces apart when she came back to herself. Oh, dear God, what had she done? That was the very thing they needed to do spiritual combat with the murderous Pilgrim Ghost, and she had just destroyed it.

She looked up at Jon, miserable and scared, not understanding anything that had just happened.

He jumped back from her a half step, until his back hit up against the refrigerator with a hollow rattling of the condiment bottles inside. His face drained of color.

"What is it?" she said, cold fingers of dread tickling up her spine. "What is it? Jon, what is it?"

"Your face," was all he said.

And then she knew.

A cry of terror caught in her throat as she raced from the kitchen, through the living room and up the stairs to where the bedrooms and the storage room and the bathroom were. It was the bathroom she needed, and she rushed in, throwing open the door so hard in her haste that it banged against the linen closet. It was a small space built in an era before huge on suites had become the fashion. The tub and the other amenities didn't leave a lot of space for the small sink. Darcy gripped the edge of the vanity to steady herself and stared into the mirrored cabinet secured to the wall in front of her.

Her reflection stared back at her. Her face.

Only, there was someone else there with her.

There was the faint outline of another person, like their image had been taken and photoshopped over her own. A man with an angular jaw and sharp cheekbones. His hair was darker than her own. Deep pools of shadow stared at her menacingly, piercing through her hazel eyes. She knew that face hovering there around her own.

It was the same face she had seen in the book at Benson LaCroix's house. Nathaniel Williams.

The Pilgrim Ghost.

"Get out of my body!" she blurted out. It was the first thing that came to her mind.

The next thing was an image of her own hands around Jon's neck, squeezing and squeezing until the life had been forced out of him.

"No!" she shrieked, knowing that Jon could hear everything she was saying downstairs. "No, I won't do that! You get out of my body. Right now!"

In the reflection, the mouth that was not hers opened wide in a cruel, inhuman laugh.

All this time she had thought it was Jon who had been possessed. Jon who had attacked her. Jon who was in danger.

Ghost Story

She'd been wrong.

It was her.

The ghost of Nathaniel Williams had taken over her body while she slept. Even as Millie had been trying to tell her how to defend herself, the entity known as the Pilgrim Ghost had stolen into her and used her own body against her. That was why her injuries weren't that bad. There was only so much a person could do to hurt themselves.

Her hand rose of its own accord, against her will, and slammed palm first into the mirror. Nathaniel Williams' hand slapped against it from the other side of the reflection. She heard the glass stress under the blow, and knew if she hit much harder it would break, sharp edged slivers cutting into her flesh. The ghost smirked at her. That was what he wanted.

There were ways for a spirit to hurt someone when they had control of them. Possessing spirits had been known to kill their victims, in rare cases.

She was in a bathroom full of chemicals and sprays and razors and other common household items that could be turned deadly with the flick of a wrist.

Her right hand pulled back and slammed forward again even as she grabbed for it with her left. This time her palm stung with the force of the blow. Tiny hairline cracks appeared around her fingers.

Blood dripped from the pad of her thumb.

Darcy had to act fast to get the entity out of her. She might never have done an exorcism of another person before, with all the complicated techniques that were involved with that—the method and the way—but Darcy knew the simple method for getting a ghost out of herself. She'd only had to use it once, when she was young and stupid and invited someone into her without realizing it, but a person didn't easily forget that sort of thing.

She heard Jon running up after her. Everything was happening so fast. Only a few seconds had passed since she'd come up here, but a few seconds was all it would take for Nathaniel Williams to end her life. She needed Jon's help now. *Right now.*

"Jon!" she called down to him. She couldn't leave the bathroom. The image in the mirror was holding her fast. Her feet felt like they had been cemented in place. "Jon, I need you to go downstairs and break the salt lines!"

His footsteps stopped halfway up the stairs. "You need me to…what now?"

Her right hand pulled back again, struggling against the grip of her left.

"I need you to break the salt lines!" she repeated. "Use a broom or your foot or your hand or whatever but break the lines! Swipe through them! As many as you can! Do it now! Do it *now!*"

She was screaming, and she was scared. When she had put down those salt lines she had thought she was building a wall to keep ghosts out. Checking Jon, finding nothing in him anymore, she had just assumed the ghost had left him and gone somewhere else. But, it had still been here. Right here inside of her. In putting down the salt, by building that wall, she hadn't protected them. All she had accomplished was to box the ghost in.

With them.

Forcing the ghost out of her wouldn't do any good if it was still trapped in the house.

Jon stumbled down the stairs with a loud thumping, and then she could hear a lot of banging down there. Hopefully he had understood her hasty directions, because she couldn't keep her arm back anymore, and she could tell this time her hand would go straight through the mirror.

There was no more time.

Locking eyes with Nathaniel Williams there in her own reflection made her feel cold and slithery inside but she found his gaze, and held it. "There you are," she said to him. "I see you. I feel you."

Her hand curled into a fist, and jerked forward, then back, then forward.

It was now or never.

"Get. Out!"

She put all of her life force behind those two words, pushed from deep within herself to force anything that was not her...*out*. There was a heavy rush of foulness that collected right in her chest and ballooned and the pressure was terrible but she kept pushing on it and exerting her will against it until in the mirror she started to see the strain on the ghost's face and she knew she was winning.

Nathaniel Williams opened his mouth, and screamed loud enough that Darcy heard it across the barrier between life and death. The lights in the bathroom dimmed. One of the energy efficient bulbs popped in a cloud of chemical dust.

Then the balled up mass of the entity that had taken up residence inside of her rushed away, leaving her dizzy and disoriented, stumbling backward and grabbing the shower curtain to keep from dumping herself into the tub.

The sound of the ghost's scream dissipated like faint echoes in the distance, and it was gone.

Darcy needed to sit down. She needed to lie down, and sleep for a week, and her stomach growled so hard that she doubled over in pain around it for a moment. Self-exorcism. It took a lot out of a girl.

There was no time to stop and rest, though. She needed to know that the ghost was actually gone, and not still in the house. If Jon had done what she asked, then they were fine. There had been enough force behind that shove she'd given Nathaniel Williams' spirit to send it half way across the spectral plains. If it wasn't still trapped in her house.

That was a big if.

"Jon!" she called out, weakly, forcing herself to move her feet and shuffle to the stairs, holding her right hand still, her life's blood leaking out of a dozen little tiny cuts. It wasn't as bad as it looked, she decided. Like a bunch of paper cuts really. That was all. She could wrap it in a towel later. Right now, she needed to know if they were safe.

Struggling downstairs, leaning heavily on the railing, she found Jon waiting for her. His face was pale. His eyes were wide as he stared at her, searching her face. Darcy knew what he was looking for.

"Is he...?" he started to ask.

Darcy swallowed and nodded. "Yes. Did you break the salt lines?"

"I think so. I've never done this before. I scuffed my feet through the lines in front of the doors. Then I wiped away some of the salt from the windows. Is that okay? I didn't know what you meant."

She made it to him, and fell into his arms, loving how he held her. "That's what I meant, Jon. Thank you. You probably saved us both." The next part was harder for her to get out of a throat dry like desert sand. "I'm sorry. Jon, I was so sure it was you. I never thought to check myself. It was me. It was me, Jon."

"Shh," he comforted her, combing her hair back from her face with his fingers. "It's all right, Darcy. I know it was you. You got rid of him. You beat him. It's over."

"No, Jon. You don't understand. It was me, here, in this house."

He scrunched up his eyebrows. "Darcy, I know. It was you. You just got rid of him."

"That's not what I mean!" She was trembling, and she held up her right hand, the sight of the blood making her nauseous. Or, maybe that was because of what she was trying to explain to Jon. "Nathaniel Williams was in me. He was possessing me. If he was in me now…"

Then maybe it was her that had killed the woman on Helen's lawn.

She saw in his eyes that he understood her, even though neither of them could say it out loud. He held her tighter, and stroked her back, and tried to keep his voice from being all choked up as he said, "It will be all right, Darcy. We'll figure it out. Won't we? That's what we always do. We figure it out. You and me. We'll figure this out."

"He's not gone," she told him. "I didn't get rid of him for good. Just got him out of me."

Somehow, that fact made everything worse.

"What are you saying?" he asked her, suddenly very still against her.

"I'm saying, we didn't stop him. I have to do the exorcism still. Oh. And we need to redo the salt trails here before his spirit gathers itself back together and comes at us again."

"How? You destroyed that page in the book. Or, he destroyed it, I mean. All I've got is the last four sentences. I checked."

She nodded against his chest, not sure if she had ever felt more scared or more safe than she did in that moment in his arms. "I tore it up to little pieces because I couldn't stop him. But, I read it first. You brought me out of my haze long enough for me to see the page. I read every word. I know the method we need to use. Thank you, Jon. You probably saved my life."

"Uh, no problem," he muttered. Then again, what do you say to someone after you've helped them break free of a vengeful spirit?

So. She knew the method of the exorcism. Even though Nathaniel Williams had tried to keep her from it by blurring her sight and clouding her mind, she had seen it and memorized it. It was complicated but she had done harder rituals before.

All she needed was the way. What was the way?

Darcy thought back to her dream. What had Millie said about the way?

Something that didn't make any sense. Something about how the way was right where it belongs and it was better off where it was. No. Not better. That wasn't the word she had used.

"Are you okay, Darcy?" Jon asked her, which she thought was a stupid question under the circumstances. "Your hand is bleeding. Let's take care of that."

"Shh," she said. "Hold on. I'm trying to remember something."

Not better. Aunt Millie had said something else. Millie had said, and it was where it needed to be now.

That wasn't it, either. Not exactly, anyway. In a dream like that, one that connected her to the realm of the dead, anything that was said could have a very specific meaning. She would need to remember the exact words if she was going to figure out what Millie had been trying to tell her.

Ghost Story

She held up her right hand, saw the blood. There didn't seem to be any glass in the cuts, which was good, but she was right handed and it was going to be a pain to have it wrapped up while she was performing an exorcism or whatever else she would need to do. Why did it need to be her right hand?

Wait.

That was it. That was what Millie had said to her. Right. She had told Darcy that the way was where it had always been, and it was right where it belonged.

On her right hand, the antique silver ring that Millie had passed down to Darcy sat in its place on her finger. On her right hand.

It was right, where it belonged.

The way. This was the way.

The ring had an odd geometrical design of curves and angles circling it, and a tiny rose crafted by some master metal smith to look so real it was like a tiny blossom had been caught in the metal itself. Darcy had often wondered at the designs on the ring. There was nothing in Millie's journal or any of her other books about it. It had simply been a unique piece of jewelry, a stunning memory of the aunt who had raised her for most of her formative years.

Only now, looking at it again in light of the communication method she had read through, she could see the ring for what it was. It was a sculpted path, a representation of the way the exorcised spirit had to be forced away from this mortal coil so that it could not find its way back.

It was the way.

Clenching her hand into a tight fist, she breathed a few silent words. "Thank you, Millie."

She knew how to do it now.

She was ready.

Chapter Seven

When Darcy had told Jon that she'd never performed an exorcism, she'd told him the truth. There had been a few people in town or as far away as Inglesburg who thought their houses were haunted and thought they needed an exorcism. Sometimes, to make them feel better, Darcy had made up a ritual cleansing on the spot. She would throw some salt, walk through the house reciting Latin or gibberish even, and then walk away declaring the house clean.

A bit dramatic, but every time she'd done it the families in those houses never had a problem with their "ghost" again. Probably because it had only been the product of an overactive imagination coupled with the sounds of a house settling.

Doing a real exorcism, on a specter as powerful as the Pilgrim Ghost, would require a lot of energy and willpower. Which was why she opted to go to bed before she fell asleep on the floor.

After repairing the salt lines and making sure all the windows and doors were locked, Darcy had stumbled. Jon had been exactly two steps behind her the whole time and had been there to catch her. In actuality, her knees had buckled from exhaustion, but she wasn't going to tell him that. He was worried about her enough as it was. She also wasn't going to argue with him when he told her to take her clothes off and get in bed.

Ghost Story

Dreams came and went, and she knew some of them came from her Aunt Millie even though she didn't appear in any of them personally. There were some about her childhood, her mother and father and sister. Smudge walked through several of them as his normal cat self. A few were close to nightmares, made up of worries about what would happen if they couldn't stop Nathaniel Williams.

If he killed anyone else.

She was watching Williams' hanging in one of the dreams. It was the scene from the painting in Benson's book, only it was so very real. She saw Williams swinging from his gallows rope. She saw the look of satisfaction on the faces of the people around him, heard the insults they hurled at him. Over in the corner, the grandfather clock ticked its way toward midnight, the second hand moving steadily around until it was right at the cusp of striking the witching hour.

Then it stopped, and the clock's mechanisms broke with a loud *sproing*.

11:59.

Nathaniel Williams stopped kicking. His body lay still and limp where it hung. He was dead.

Through the crowd came Whitmarsh Grace. Darcy had never seen a picture of him but she knew instinctively that this was her distant ancestor, the man who had sent Nathaniel Williams to his death. He was tall and lean, with the hard look of someone who would just as soon shoot you now and ask questions of your corpse. He tipped a wide black hat to another man in the crowd, a portly gentleman in a black coat with long tails who gave the impression of being the leader of the group.

A wooden ladder was brought forth and Whitmarsh climbed up to the beam that supported the dead man on his rope. From his belt he unsheathed a long, thick knife and Darcy thought the dream would show him cutting Nathaniel Williams down. Instead, he began carving into the beam. Intricate designs that matched the ones in the painting. The same pattern in her ring.

"What art thou about up there, Whitmarsh?" the portly man asked.

"Can't risk that his spirit might hold us ill," Whitmarsh answered. "I know a bit of spellwork from my mother. This will keep his spirit from finding his way back and haunting us here."

In the dream, Darcy looked down at the ring on her hand. Whitmarsh's carvings were close. Close, but he had missed a vital line. Without that one part of the way, Whitmarsh's ghost would be free to come back. Darcy's ancestor had made a mistake.

Now they were dealing with the results.

After that she slept soundly for hours. The dreams were all done. Whatever they had to tell her had already been told and she was left to herself for a while. Eventually she woke up from that peaceful, dark oblivion, slowly coming around enough to realize it was one o'clock in the afternoon. When it dawned on her that it was a week day, she sat up in a panic, thinking about how her store needed to be opened and she needed to check on Grace and Aaron and Helen and...

"Ohh," she groaned, not sure if her stomach or her head hurt worse. The aches in her muscles were just faint reminders of something she'd rather forget. Her right hand had been wrapped in gauze that showed faint spots of red here and there. Everything else was tolerable, but her stomach and her skull were holding Olympic tryouts to see which could cause her the most grief. The judges were still conferring.

Darcy studied her hand, with the makeshift bandage on it, and smiled at Jon's handiwork. Not bad. The cuts would heal over quickly and she still had use of her hand even though two of the fingers were bandaged up like a mummy's. She looked over her ring again, seeing the way etched into it even better now that her mind was clearer.

"There you are." Jon's voice sounded relieved as he stopped to lean in the bedroom door. He was wearing dark dress pants and a blue shirt with a stiff collar. Work clothes. He noticed her looking him over. "I had to go into the station this morning. I wanted to know where they were with the investigation. Chief Daleson told me to take the rest of the day off, though. I told him you weren't feeling well. He didn't argue with me."

"Gee, thanks," she said, happy that she could provide him with an excuse to play hooky. She couldn't disagree with what he'd said, though. She felt horrible. "I need to check in with my job, too. I have a bookstore to run, you know."

"Izzy has it," he told her, meaning her one and only employee. "I talked to her this morning. She's got everything covered."

Darcy knew she could trust Izzy. She'd come to rely on her friend more and more since they'd started working together. Now that she knew the store was covered, she could focus on other things.

Like how empty her stomach was.

A loud rumbling in her belly was followed by cramps that twisted her insides. "Unh," she complained. "I need to eat. Like, a lot. But I want to check on Grace and the others first. They need to know what's going on. About the ghost, I mean. And, well, me."

About her being moved up to number one on the suspect list, she kept herself from adding out loud.

"It's okay," Jon said to her. He stepped away from the door and came to sit down next to her on the bed. Darcy didn't know if maybe he was speaking to her silent fears. "I invited everyone here for dinner. I figured that way we'd all be together in one place, and we could let everyone know what happened."

"You didn't tell them yet?"

He shrugged. "It didn't seem like the kind of thing to talk about over the phone."

"Good point." Her stomach growled at her again. "Um. Maybe I could get a snack before dinner?"

Leaning in to kiss her cheek, he finally smiled. "For you, Sweet Baby, anything."

Her nickname from his lips made her feel a little better. Even in the middle of a dangerous situation that none of them could tell anyone about, she and Jon could remain a strong team.

They had made it past their rough patch, when everything seemed to be going wrong for them. Bad choices, egos, fate. All of it. Now that they were back together they could face anything.

"Come on," he said. "I'll help you downstairs. Then I'll make you the best turkey sandwich you've ever had."

Jon had asked that everyone meet at five o'clock, a little earlier than they usually had dinner but it seemed like a good idea to have everyone together before the sun started to set. Darcy had to agree with him. She doubted any of them would be comfortable out in the dark of night. Not now.

Not that it mattered. Grace and Aaron dropped by shortly after three o'clock. Aaron looked a little sheepish, and Grace tried to explain it away by saying she was dying to know what was going on with the investigation down at the police station. Darcy knew better, though.

They spaced themselves out on the couch and in the two comfortable easy chairs in the living room. They'd replaced their old chairs just last week, and these new ones were gray suede, comfortable and homey. Aaron almost fell into one, his eyes drooping heavily.

"He's been up all night," Grace explained in a whisper as she handed baby Addison over to sit in her auntie Darcy's lap. "He wouldn't even come lay down in bed."

"I was worried," Aaron said. "And I'm tired, not deaf."

Grace rolled her eyes, but Darcy could tell that she loved Aaron for wanting to protect her and their new baby.

While Grace and Jon discussed the details of Bonnie Verhault's death, at least as far as the officers of the Misty Hollow Police Department understood them, Darcy rocked Addison gently in her arms. Such a pretty baby. Grace and Aaron had done a great thing in bringing this little life into the world. She couldn't help but think that maybe she and Jon could do the same, soon, if their plans for the wedding ever fleshed themselves out.

She was reminded again of that moment during Nathaniel Williams' manifestation at Helen's house when she had been sure that baby Addison was communicating with her. There had been this sensation of hearing someone speaking, crying out for help, and it hadn't been any of the adults. Had she imagined it?

In the hospital, when Grace had just given birth and Darcy had seen Addison for the first time, there had been this instant sense of connection between them. After considering that feeling from every possible angle Darcy had come to a single conclusion. It seemed the family gift had been passed down to Grace's baby. Addison had a connection to the paranormal just like Darcy did.

That little fact was something that Darcy was still keeping secret, waiting for a good time to let Grace know what her baby would become, but it was just as much a part of Addison as her ten fingers and ten toes were. So, if this beautiful little baby had that gift, why shouldn't she be able to communicate with Darcy? Even if it was only telepathically.

"Can you hear me, Addison?" she whispered, looking into the child's wide blue eyes. "Can you talk to Aunt Darcy?"

"Sis?" Grace asked her, interrupting her efforts to reach out to Addison. "You okay?"

"Sure," she said quickly. "Just having a moment with my niece. What were we talking about?"

"What else?" Grace said wryly. "We're talking about that dead girl. Jon says that the guys down at the station have notified her next of kin and touched base with her employer. She was here in Misty Hollow on business, scouting a location for a client. A land purchase."

"Right." Darcy picked up the explanation from there. "The whole deal with Nathaniel Williams is that he thought all of the area in and around Misty Hollow belonged to him. He felt strongly enough about it to get himself hung fighting over it. It makes sense that his ghost has the same unresolved issues."

"Okay, fine, I'll play along," Grace said, nervously pulling at the tips of her fingers. "This ghost has problems. Big, major problems that make him homicidal." She saw the look Darcy gave her and quickly added, "This is your area, Darcy. I'm not doubting you. It's just a lot to swallow. Anyway. The ghost wants everyone to pay for being mean to him and taking away his property. Fine. Why is he coming out now? Why not a hundred years ago? Or fifty or ten, or whatever. Why now?"

"That's a good question," Darcy said. "I'm not sure I know the whole answer, but I think it has something to do with history. There are families in Misty Hollow who are descendants of the original settlers. Williams' group. It turns out, the elected lawman who arrested and then hung Williams was our ancestor. Whitmarsh Grace. You know that whole thing about mom's side of the family descending from the Streeters, who descended from the Graces?"

Her sister nodded along with the story. "I remember. Wow. I didn't realize law enforcement went that far back in our family tree."

Darcy tickled baby Addison's chin and managed a laugh. "All the way back to the beginning. Guess it's in your genes. So, if he's coming out now, it might have something to do with our connection to the town's history. If enough pieces fall back into place, it can raise a troubled spirit. Whitmarsh Grace was the lawman at the time, you're in law enforcement now. Plus I'm engaged to Jon, and I get myself involved in his work more often than not."

"Thankfully for me," Jon added.

Darcy stuck her tongue out at him before continuing. "So there's that, but also there's how Williams believed the town was stolen from him way back then, and how someone is buying up land in the town now. There's a lot of parallels in play here and I'm betting there's even more to it. Another connection or two that tugged at the Pilgrim Ghost somehow."

"That's all well and good," Jon said, "but it doesn't help us. For whatever reason, he's here now, and we need to stop him. Darcy has figured out a way to do it."

He explained everything that had happened to them here as quickly as he could. The book, Darcy's possession, all of it. When he was done, the room was as silent as a tomb. Even Aaron sat up wide eyed, his exhaustion forgotten.

"Wow, sis," Grace said at last. "That's...I don't know what to call what that is."

"Saying it sucks just about covers it," she offered.

"That's why you've got the salt laid out across your doorstep?" Grace looked over at the living room windows to see the salt lines there, too. She knew enough about Darcy's gift to know what that meant. "You know, I nearly stepped in that. You could warn a person."

"So when do we do this ritual?" Aaron asked. "If we have a way to stop this thing, then let's do it."

"We will," Darcy assured him. "But we need to do it at the Town Hall. And we'll need to do it when no one else is around. So, we'll have to wait until tonight."

"Great," Grace muttered, pretty much summing up what all of them were thinking.

"Why the Town Hall?" Aaron asked. "You can't just do it from here? Aren't we protected from that...ghost, as long as we're in this house?"

Darcy wished it were that simple. "We are, but the thing is we need to do the ritual where the ghost has taken up residence. He's floating around town freely right now—"

"And hitching rides in people," Jon said bitterly.

"Right. That too. But his manifestation is centered in the Town Hall. I've felt him there any number of times. I think Helen has felt it, too. She's been spending a lot of time there lately, and she's been acting strange. I've heard her talking to people in her office and when I go in there's no one there. She kept saying it was a phone call, and I believed her because I wanted to. I didn't put it together until now but I think the Pilgrim Ghost has been talking to her. Influencing her somehow."

"Possessing her," Jon summarized. "We saw her at lunch yesterday. The ghost was in her just like it was in you."

"Darcy…" Grace started to say, then stopped.

It was easy for Darcy to read her sister's thoughts whether she spoke them out loud or not. They were written all over her face. "It's all right, Grace. Yes, I know what that means. Helen and I both have been possessed by Nathaniel Williams. Either of us could be the actual killer. I don't like how that adds up, but there it is."

"No," Jon said emphatically. "There's no way you did that. The preliminary autopsy showed that each knife stroke was made with a lot of force. Not only do I not believe you're capable of killing anyone, possessed or not, but I'm not sure you'd have the strength to do this."

Her smile was bittersweet. "I'm stronger than I look, you know. Plus, a person who is possessed can have unnatural strength, augmented by the ghost's presence. So. Don't count me out."

He reached across to her with his hand, and she took it, grateful for his faithful trust. It didn't change the facts, but just knowing he would stand by her no matter what made her feel better.

"Where is Helen, anyway?" Grace said. "I figured her and Andrew would have been camped out on your door step, Darcy. Another murder in her town, and on her front lawn, no less."

Darcy knew this must be hard on Helen as the town's mayor. The first leader of the town had been cursed by Nathaniel Williams. Now Helen had been used by him to deliver a deadly message, one that had come true right in front of her own house.

Hmm. Maybe that was the other connection. Darcy would have to ask Helen as soon as she—

"There they are," Jon said, craning his neck to look out the window. "I can see Andrew driving, too. Good. We should all be together for this. Right now, we're the only ones who know what's really happening. I want to keep it that way. We need a good plan, a strong plan, and we need to stick to it."

Grace tapped her hand against Darcy's shoulder. "Don't you just love it when he gets like this?"

Letting some heat into her voice, Darcy lowered her eyelashes. "Oh, yeah I do. It was one of the first things that attracted me to him."

"Sure it was," Jon snorted. "Why don't you guys stay here and I'll go let them in."

"Hold on," Darcy said, handing baby Addison back to her mom. "I'll come with you."

Helen was already at the front door, knocking once to be courteous and then coming on in. She looked even more tired than Aaron did and Darcy could easily imagine that she had been up all night pacing back and forth while Andrew tried to convince her to get some sleep. Helen was very dedicated to this town. Darcy had seen her sacrifice herself over and over for the people who lived here.

Hopefully, she would be able to continue doing just exactly that.

"Hi Darcy," she greeted them with a warm smile that did nothing to ease the dark circles under her eyes. "Hi Jon. I see Grace and Aaron are already here? Andrew's right behind me. So. Let's get started, shall we?"

"Actually, we've already started." Darcy took Helen's dark knee-length tweed jacket with the big blue buttons and hung it up next to the door. Even Helen's clothes looked tired, a rumpled white blouse and black slacks that could have been described as slept in if Darcy hadn't already decided her friend had gotten no sleep at all. "Why don't you come on into the living room and we'll fill you in on what we know before we have something to eat."

"Oh, I don't think I have much of an appetite," Helen assured her. "Just thinking that one of us could have killed that poor girl. That it could have been me!"

She looked down at her shaking hands, then wiped them on the front of her slacks as if she could wipe away traces of imaginary blood. Not that she should be, but Darcy could see Helen wasn't taking this well at all.

Imaginary blood. That was one of the things Darcy planned on doing tonight, was performing the ritual to check each of them for guilt. Blood on their hands. If nothing else, it would rule out intentional murder.

"What's this?" Helen was asking. She was looking down at the floor in front of the door.

"Oh, that's salt," Darcy said matter-of-factly. "If you put it in place the right way then it keeps spirits from entering your home. It's like a no trespassing sign."

"Oh," was Helen's response. "Well, so long as it keeps that thing away from us."

"Actually, there's been some developments in that," Darcy said, hating that she would have to start this story all over again. It might make Helen feel better to know someone else had gone through what she had, but Darcy was not proud of herself for allowing Williams to possess her.

Andrew came up on the porch then, smiling at Jon and Darcy and reaching out for Helen. "You need to sit down, dear," he said to her, "before you drop."

"Oh, don't be such a worrywart," Helen said to him, although she smiled wider when she did, and maybe stood a little straighter.

Andrew's smile slipped, and he let his hand drop to his side, standing there on the porch, not quite inside yet. "Uh, I'm sorry. I forgot something in the car. Go on in, Helen. I won't be long."

"Okay," she said, although he had already turned away and down the steps. "But hurry!"

Jon took Helen into the living room while Darcy went into the kitchen to make tea and coffee. She couldn't remember which Aaron liked but Jon and Grace were both coffee drinkers. Wasn't Helen? What about Andrew? She couldn't remember. She'd have to ask. While she set the kettle to boil she went over in her mind everything she would need to do tonight during the exorcism ritual. Everything she would need was already here. Her candles. Her ring, showing her the way to follow while pushing Nathaniel Williams out of this realm, salt and powdered rue and basil leaf in her baking cabinet…

Oops. For Pete's sake, she was out of salt. She'd used everything she had to guard her house against Nathaniel Williams. Well, that was one of the great things about living in a town like Misty Hollow. She could always go up to any of her neighbors' houses and ask for a cup of salt.

She just wouldn't tell them what she needed it for. Not unless she wanted them to call the hospital and have a room reserved for her in the mental ward.

A thought came to her. It started out small, then grew until it was demanding her attention. A bad, dark thought that she pushed away more than once. It refused to be banished no matter how hard she tried.

The salt. The line of salt across the floor.

GHOST STORY

Her heart froze. Ghosts wouldn't cross the lines she had laid out. Not across a hearth. A living space like a home always accumulated energies, over time, from the people who lived there. That energy, in turn, created a sort of power that someone with Darcy's gifts could tap into. Salt itself was just salt. Salt fueled by the power of a living space, when put down properly, created a barrier no ghost could ever cross.

Andrew had kept himself from crossing over the threshold of the front door just now.

What if…oh, dear God, what if the Pilgrim Ghost had found a new host in Andrew?

She rushed to the door even as the teakettle started to whistle and threw it wide open, ready for anything.

Andrew stood there, his hand held out for the doorknob, a surprised look on his face. "Oh. Uh, thanks for getting the door Darcy. Helen in the living room?"

And then he walked past her, into the house, across the salt line.

Darcy let out a breath and slumped back against the wall. Taking a few deep breaths to steady herself she pushed off the wall and headed back into the kitchen. She had been thinking the worst. It hadn't been true, but she was still on edge. Anyone could be in danger of the Pilgrim Ghost taking them over, using them to do who knew what, and none of them would ever know until bad things were already happening. Like with the book on exorcisms. Or worse, the murder at Helen's.

A soft rapping on the doorway between the living room and the kitchen snapped her attention away from her spiraling thoughts. Helen stood there, an apologetic look on her face, tears in her eyes. "Oh, Darcy. I had no idea what had happened to you. I'm so, so sorry."

In the livingroom Jon's cell phone rang.

Darcy took her friend by the hands and brought her over to the kitchen table to sit down. "Helen, it's hardly your fault. You couldn't have known what was going on, let alone stop it."

Helen shook her head. "I can't help thinking if I'd been stronger, then maybe that girl would still be alive." She looked up at Darcy, her lower lip starting to tremble. "It wasn't any ghost who killed her. It was a human hand. Whether I believe this whole possession thing or not, and I'm not saying I do, there was still a murder committed. One of us six did it. It's starting to look like it was either you, or me. We're the ones who have been through… you know. Being used like that. So which one of us do you think it was?"

That was the question, wasn't it? Was there any way to prove it conclusively, either way? Regressive hypnosis, maybe. Maybe calling on the ghost of the dead girl, if Darcy could get close enough to the corpse. Jon had already told her that there wasn't any trace evidence on the body. No hairs, no fibers, nothing that pointed to anyone in particular. The prevailing theory at the station was that Bonnie Verhault was killed by someone who didn't want the sale of the land to go through, possibly a rival company, and the body dumped on the mayor's lawn as a warning.

Well. They were closer to the truth than they realized.

"Helen," she started, letting out a long breath. "I think…"

Jon burst into the kitchen, going for his shoes. "Darcy, something's happened downtown. I need to go into the station. You need to come with me."

Helen and Darcy were both on their feet. "What happened?" Darcy asked him.

He hesitated for just a second before answering, carefully not looking at Helen. "That was Chief Daleson. He wants me down at the station now. With you, Darcy."

"What? Why?"

"He wouldn't say. That's what worries me."

There was no doubt in Darcy's mind that this wasn't a coincidence. This was the ghost trying to distract them.

Trying to draw them out.

"We need to go," Jon told her, offering his hand to help her out of the chair. "I have the feeling if we don't go now he'll send someone to get us."

"Fine. Helen, stay here with everyone. You'll be safe here in the house. We'll be back as soon as we can."

The question of who the killer was, the physical killer whose hand had swung the knife, would have to wait.

Unless the police had found something after all.

That thought didn't make her feel any better.

Chapter Eight

The police station interview room had never seemed so cold, or so scary. With its gray walls and poured concrete floor it had never been an inviting space, but now that Darcy was experiencing what it felt like firsthand, she hoped to never come in here again. Ever. She and Jon sat at the metal table in the room's center, side by side. The chair on the other side was empty. No one had come in to speak to them in nearly twenty minutes.

Staring down at the stainless steel rings set in the table's surface, meant for handcuffing suspects to, Darcy clenched and unclenched her fists and tried to remain calm. "I thought you said the Chief told you this was urgent?"

"He did," Jon promised. "I don't like this. This is how I treat a suspect. Leave them to sweat a little, then come in with some unexpected information to gauge their reaction."

Darcy had seen him do it, too. She knew he was right. "Maybe we should go? I mean, we're not under arrest are we?"

He took her hand in his on top of the table. "Not a good idea. Let's just wait and see what he wants from us."

Leaving still seemed like a good idea to her. She was about to tell him so when the door to the interview room opened and Chief Joe Daleson came in with a distracted smile.

Ghost Story

"Sorry to make you two wait," he told them. "I wanted to check this information myself before I discussed it with you."

He was carrying a manila folder, full of papers, and he set it down on the table in front of them without opening it. The sleeves of his white button up shirt were rolled up to his elbows. His red tie had been badly knotted and hung unevenly. His expression was stony and hard to read. In short, he looked like a man who would rather be anywhere but where he was right now.

Scratching at his balding scalp, he looked directly at Jon. "I'm not happy about this. I want you to know that up front."

Darcy tensed. That was not a promising opening line. She couldn't help but notice how the folder was marked with the dead girl's name. If he had called them down to talk about this, and if he was opening with an apology, then what was coming had to be bad news.

Jon held her hand tighter, but kept his voice even. "What's up, Chief? Did you get a break in the case?"

"Sort of, yes," he said, with a skeptical glance at Jon. "This doesn't look good, let me tell you."

"Chief, can I just say—" Darcy sucked in a sharp breath to keep from yelping as Jon just about broke her knuckles squeezing her hand.

"Darcy, let's listen to what the Chief has to say. I know you're in a rush to get back home, but I'm sure that can wait."

"Yes," she said, knowing what Jon was telling her. She needed to be quiet and see what Joe had to tell them first. She could confess or lie or ask for a lawyer after that. Trusting Jon was the best thing she could do right now.

The Chief tapped his finger against the folder a few times, considering what he had just seen pass between Darcy and Jon. "Right. Well. Here's why I asked you two to come in. I went back out to the scene today at Helen's house with Wilson and a few others. It didn't make sense to me that we hadn't found the murder weapon yet. Couple of other things not sitting right with me on this one, either."

That was an understatement, Darcy thought.

From the folder, he slid an eight-by-ten sized photograph. He must have had it placed so that he could take it out without looking. His eyes never left Darcy and Jon as he removed it and placed it on the table between them.

"This is what I found," he said.

The photo showed one of the officers holding back the bushes at Helen's property. On the ground, half buried in the dirt, was a knife with blood on the handle, and on the blade, and even in the photograph it was easy to see that there were fingerprints dried into the red splotches.

"Don't know why we didn't find it yesterday." He turned the photograph so that it was facing him, and pointed at the handle. "See this right here? You know what that is?"

"It's a fingerprint, Chief," Jon said, his tone flat.

Darcy nodded, not trusting her voice. There it was. Proof that one of them was the killer. Helen, or her, or maybe even one of the others although that was less likely. She could feel perspiration beading at the back of her neck.

"Yes, fingerprints," the Chief said with a smile. "We'll know who did this for sure soon enough. For right now, I've got my suspicions."

He looked at Darcy as he said it, and she very nearly blurted out a confession right there, whether she was certain of her guilt or not. Instead, she followed Jon's subtle advice and stayed quiet.

"Thing is," Joe continued, "it takes time for the hotshots at the state crime lab to get any kind of match on fingerprints. A

GHOST STORY

whole day, maybe more. So I went looking for other evidence. That's what good cops do. Right, Detective Tinker?"

This time his eyes levelled themselves at Jon. Darcy was proud of the way Jon didn't buckle under that steely gaze.

"I agree with you, Chief. I'm sorry I haven't been around much for this one. Darcy hasn't been feeling well."

"So you told me," was the non-committal response. "Tell me, Jon, when you discovered the body at the scene did you check the contents of her purse?"

Darcy turned to Jon. She hadn't heard anything about there being a purse at the scene. Jon ignored her, but she could tell that he noticed her looking at him.

"No," he told the Chief. "I didn't want to disturb the scene. I know how it looked. All of us were there while the body was being dumped. If I was investigating this one then I'd suspect one of us. I wasn't going to go rummaging around the scene and make it look like I was tampering with evidence."

That seemed to make Joe relax, if just a little. "That makes sense. I hadn't looked at it like that, Jon. Just couldn't help but wonder why you missed this."

He took out another photograph in the same way, slipping it easily out of the folder and setting it on top of the picture of the murder weapon. This one was a close up of a cell phone lying on a table. It was an iPhone, but not one of the newer models.

"That the victim's phone?" Jon asked.

"Yes, it is." Joe took out another piece of paper from the folder. This time it was a report of some sort with numbers listed in neat rows all down the page. "It wasn't locked. Don't know why people do that, just leave their phones open that way for anyone to get in. Glad she did, though. This is a partial list of phone calls made from her phone. We tracked down each of the numbers, and we found one that she was calling repeatedly. Over and over."

Darcy caught herself blinking, her mouth falling open. Phone calls? Darcy hadn't gotten any phone calls from Bonnie Verhault. That meant Joe didn't suspect her. So if not her, then he must suspect…

Helen.

"See this number right here?" he asked Jon. "Turns out that's the number to the Town Hall. The mayor's office, to be precise."

He waited a moment for that to sink in.

"Chief," Jon said, "you can't really suspect the mayor herself?"

"I'm sorry, both of you. I know Helen is a good friend but I have to go where the evidence leads me. This knife here," he said, shuffling the photos to put the bloody knife back on top, "appears to come from Helen's house. We found a matching set in her kitchen."

"It could be a common type," Jon pointed out. "Maybe it's sold everywhere from WalMart to K-Mart to the dollar stores. There's no way of knowing it came from Helen's drawers, I'm guessing?"

Chief Daleson put a finger up and began shaking it for emphasis. "See, that's why I asked you to come down for this, Jon. You always think of the hard angles. Like that. Now, that was a good point. We don't know for sure where the knife came from." He scratched his scalp again. "But if you add together the other evidence, it does not look good for Helen. The phone calls to her office, for instance."

"It doesn't mean she ever spoke to our victim," Jon argued. "One of the secretaries could have fielded those calls."

"Not likely," Joe said with a shake of his head. "Not that many of them."

"Okay, true, it's unlikely, but that doesn't mean it couldn't have happened that way."

Drumming his fingers, Joe nodded. "You're right, of course. That's all circumstantial. Nothing that we could convict on. We'll have to wait for that fingerprint report to come back before we can be sure of a conviction. We do have enough to make an arrest right now, and that's what I wanted your opinion on, Jon. This is the mayor we're talking about. The mayor of the entire town of Misty Hollow. No good can come of arresting the mayor, especially after we had to arrest her husband, who was mayor at the time himself. The people of this town have had enough of scandal and murder to last them a lifetime and I don't want to add more to that. Not without good, solid evidence to back it up."

"So," Jon said, slowly, "you're asking my opinion?"

"That's why I brought you down here." The Chief spread his hands wide like the point should have been obvious, and then leaned back in his chair.

Darcy heard the long sigh of breath Jon let escape through his nose. Joe probably missed it, but Darcy knew Jon well enough to sense the waves of relief rolling off him. He and Darcy hadn't been called down here for one of them to be arrested. Not only that, but Jon had the chance to keep any charges from being brought against Helen.

At least for now.

"Chief, I don't think we have enough yet. We should get the fingerprint evidence, and maybe even bring Helen in for an official written statement."

"That might raise a few eyebrows," Joe said. "I'm trying to avoid that."

"All right. Let me do it, then. I can be quiet about it and nobody will have to see her being brought down here to the station."

Joe considered the idea, shook his head slightly. After a few moments of silence where he seemed to have an internal argument with himself he turned to Darcy. "I asked you to come down, too, because I know Helen is a good friend of yours. You've helped us out more times than I can count, Darcy, and I trust your opinion." He paused to take a deep breath. "If I went to Helen myself, just to talk, what do you think she'd do?"

Darcy had to untie the knots in her tongue before she could speak. "You mean, do I think she'll try to run away? No. Of course not. She'd welcome the chance to speak to you if it means clearing her name."

The frown that stole over Joe's face was telling. "I'm glad to hear that, Darcy, but I really think it's only a matter of time before I end up arresting her for this. I'm just delaying the inevitable. Lining up all my ducks in a row before I do anything."

"I think that's smart, Chief," Jon said quickly. "You don't want to look like you're going after an innocent woman."

Subtle, Darcy thought. Still, it did the trick. Chief Daleson nodded along to the thoughts in his head until he came to his conclusion. "Thanks. Both of you. I'll try to put a rush on the fingerprinting guys, and in the meantime I'll call and arrange a meeting with Helen. Either of you know where she is?"

"I'm not sure," Darcy lied.

"All right. I'll get ahold of her by phone. I don't suppose I have to tell the two of you not to mention anything about this to Helen, right?"

"Of course not," Jon told him. Darcy recognized the lie in his voice. "We'll keep this to ourselves. Anything else we can do to help?"

"Actually, there might be," Joe told him. He collected the photos back into the folder, making all the pages nice and neat and square before closing it up again. "Can I get both of you to stay here for just a bit longer? There's one other thing I'd like you to see."

Darcy tried to check her My Little Pony watch without being obvious about it. The interview rooms didn't have clocks in them on purpose, but she was very aware of how late it was getting. She needed to get to the Town Hall and perform the ritual. It had already been getting dark when they drove into town, and Jon's headlights had reflected off wispy tendrils of fog crawling out of the shadows and dark places. The mists, rolling heavy and thick, feeding off the trouble that had come to town.

The trouble her aunt had warned her about.

"We had someplace to be, Chief," Jon said carefully, "and you've had us here for over an hour as it is."

Joe held up a hand in an apologetic way. "Sorry. I know I'm taking up a lot of your time. I could really use your help, though. This is a big one for our town. One more in a long string of big ones, I suppose. Sort of makes a man think about retirement."

He looked at Jon as he said it, and Darcy had the feeling that there was more to his words than just idle conversation.

"Anyway. Jon, Darcy, I think you'll be able to help me with this other thing. Give me one more minute?"

Jon didn't look at Darcy, but she felt him hesitate, trying to figure some way to get her out of here so she could go and perform the exorcism and put an end to this whole mess. There really wasn't much they could do without looking suspicious. Asking the Chief to excuse them for a moment while they went and cleansed the Town Hall of a psychopathic ghost probably wouldn't go over very well.

So, finally, Jon smiled and eased back into his seat. "Sure thing. You know I'm always here for you and the department."

"That's what I like to hear," Joe said with a broad smile. He got up from the table, collecting the folder as he did. "Just be a minute."

Jon waited for the door to the interview room to close before he turned to Darcy, head very close to hers, and whispered, "We need to warn Helen."

"We need to get out of here, Jon," was her response. "I can't do anything from in here!"

"What if I could get you into a private room?" he asked in hushed tones. "If you locked the door and did the ritual here, would it still work?"

"Maybe. But, I don't have any of my supplies. Plus, the Pilgrim Ghost isn't here. He's somewhere out there in town doing God alone knows what! I need to go to where I'm sure the ghost will be."

"What, our house?"

She shook our head. "No. The Town Hall. That's where his spirit will be rooted in this world. It's the surest, safest bet."

"Okay. So, we stay here and see what the Chief has for us, then get out of here." He looked uncomfortable, and his hands held both of hers like he was afraid to let go. "It's going to be full night by the time we get out of here. I'm not comfortable with you taking this thing on at night."

"I don't know if we have a choice," she argued. "Halloween is tomorrow. That means tonight is the night that Nathaniel Williams was killed all those years ago. If I don't stop him now, I don't know how strong he might get."

He blinked at her. "That another law of ghosts?"

"Yes. It's just as true as the law of gravity, believe me."

"I do, Darcy, I do." He sat back up, looking up into the corner of the ceiling where an inconspicuous black plastic bubble sat suspended from the tiles. A surveillance camera. "Good. The red light is off. If it were on then it would be recording. Since it's not..."

He took out his cell phone and hit the first speed dial. Their house. It didn't take long for the call to get answered.

"Helen, it's Jon. Stay in the house," Darcy heard him say, still keeping his voice down. "Don't answer the phone unless it's my personal cell number."

After listening for a few seconds, he shook his head. "No. But the Chief suspects you, and the longer we can keep you away from him the better. It will give us a chance to stop the ghost and maybe prove who the killer is or isn't on our own. What's that? No. Don't worry about what the Chief told us. Helen. Don't worry. Seriously. It's nothing. I'll tell you all about it when we get back. Okay? All right. Stay inside, don't answer the door, and don't answer your phones. Unless it's me or Darcy," he added.

After a quick goodbye he hung up and put the cell phone back in his pocket. Darcy eyed him levelly until he shrugged. "What?"

"You lied to Helen just now. The evidence they have against her isn't nothing. It's a lot."

"I know."

"I mean, you did a good job of playing it down to Joe, but you've arrested people on less."

"I know," Jon repeated. "Just, give me a moment to be glad it's not you, okay?"

Darcy couldn't quite bring herself to smile. The evidence showed it wasn't her. That was something to be happy about, but not at the cost of her friend being arrested. Especially for something that wasn't her fault.

"I don't get the phone calls to her office, though," Jon said, looking around nervously, waiting for the door to open up again at any moment. "Why wouldn't Helen just tell us that she'd spoken to the victim before?"

"She probably didn't know. Remember, people who are possessed don't always remember what they've done. It's just possible that Bonnie Verhault spoke to the Pilgrim Ghost all those times, thinking it was Helen. Who knows, maybe Helen actually was on the phone some of the times I heard her in her office, just like the phone records show on that list we saw."

He took a slow breath. "That evidence is going to bury her."

"Looks like." Darcy hated this. After everything Helen had gone through, she didn't deserve to have this happen to her.

That thought had occurred to her before, and she tried to follow it through now. Did the Pilgrim Ghost somehow think Helen *did* deserve what was happening to her? Was that why he had waited all these years to come out of hiding?

Was there a connection with Helen, too?

The photographs that Chief Daleson had shown them came back to her mind. There was a lot of evidence against Helen. No jury in the world would find her innocent with all of that. The knife, especially. A bloody knife with fingerprints on it. Did it get any more damaging than that?

Not that they had the fingerprint match yet, but it was only a matter of time. Darcy clenched her teeth angrily. If it hadn't been for that bloody knife, there would be nothing to worry about. There was no real, hard evidence without that. None of them had woken up with blood on them anywhere. No one but Helen. Great, even more evidence to convict her. Yup. A jury would have a field day with all this. A victim stabbed and bloody and lying on Helen's lawn...

GHOST STORY

As something clicked into place in her mind, Darcy sat up straighter, her eyes wide.

"What is it? Are you all right?" he asked, searching her face. She knew what he was looking for. "Darcy, you aren't...I mean, he's not...you aren't...?"

"No, I'm not possessed," she said impatiently. "I just thought of something."

"What? Can it help Helen?"

"Yes." She looked up into his amazing blue eyes and managed a joyless smile. "I know who the killer is."

And that was when the lights went out.

⁓

"What's going on?" Darcy heard the note of fear in her voice. She wasn't a scaredy-cat but there was nothing natural about the lights going out in a police station, all at once, while they were there to investigate a murder committed by a ghost. Nothing at all.

A little fear was normal. Under the circumstances, she didn't mind being normal.

An emergency light, a pale red thing that didn't help them see so much as it deepened the shadows in the room, winked on over the door. It was better than nothing, Darcy supposed.

"Stay here," Jon told her. He knocked his chair over backward as he fumbled his way to his feet. "I'll be right back."

As soon as he opened the door, someone screamed.

A cold tingling spread over Darcy's skin, crawling up her spine to a spot just between her shoulder blades, making every muscle in her body tense up. She'd never been a big believer in coincidence. There could be no doubt in her mind what was going on.

"He's here," Jon guessed, echoing her thoughts. "Isn't he?"

Darcy swallowed back the lump in her throat and nodded. "We need to go. Now."

"He'll be after you," Jon guessed. "We can use the back entrance. My car's right outside."

It was a good plan. Darcy liked that plan. Of course, every plan they made usually went wrong somehow. She doubted this time would be any different.

Out into the hallway, where more red emergency lights cast their ghastly glow, Darcy followed close at Jon's heels. They kept hold of each other's hands as they went. She saw Jon reach for the gun he wasn't wearing out of habit, and she didn't have the heart to tell him it wouldn't have done him any good anyway.

Another scream. A man's voice, but high pitched and strained. Someone up towards the front of the station had found some reason to cry out in fright.

Or pain.

They made it through the hallways, down past the holding cells, to the back of the building. When they were fifty feet away from the exit door they heard the gunshots. Two, in rapid succession, followed by a lot of raised voices and shouting.

Jon stopped suddenly. "I should go see what's happening."

He turned back, still holding Darcy's hand. She tugged him closer to her. She had the eerie feeling, almost a premonition, that if she let him go down those darkened hallways that he would never come back.

Into the faint red light a figure appeared. Darcy's heart stopped. A darker shape among the shadows, it came stumbling against the walls and then turned toward her and Jon.

Ghost Story

That's when Darcy saw his face. Chief Daleson was scared. She thought nothing could ever scare this man but his eyes were darting everywhere and his chest heaved in short, quick breaths and his hand held a snub nosed automatic pistol up and ready.

His eyes locked on Jon, surprised to see him and Darcy still here. "Jon, get her out of here. I'm not sure what's going on. There's someone in the station. The lights are all out and I can't get anyone to answer me. Something's going on and…just get her out. Get her out!"

Another scream from up front was cut abruptly short. That seemed to decide things for Jon.

"Come on," he said, turning and running for the door as fast as he could.

Darcy didn't argue. She could feel the presence coming for her. Feel the dark energy of a malevolent spirit rampaging through the halls of the police station, searching for her, hunting her, tearing through everything to find her.

Out into the night, everything was dark and still. The air felt fresher than she would have thought possible, and she filled her lungs with it as they ran.

Turning, she caught a glimpse through the door, just before it closed, of a formless shadow bearing down on Joe Daleson.

Chapter Nine

They got into their car and Jon started the engine and was backing away from the police station even before he had his door closed. "I'm going to get you back to the house where I know you're safe and them I'm coming back here to help."

"Jon, no."

"Darcy, I have to. I can't leave my people, my friends, like that!"

"That's not what I meant," she explained gently. "I can't go home. Not now. I need to get to the Town Hall."

He stopped the car in the middle of the street, the tires locking up and screeching against the pavement. "What? You said you don't have any of your equipment. You said he'd be seriously strong tonight. That's what you said. What are you going to do, go in there and push the ghost out with your bare hands?"

"Of course not. Jon, look at the town."

He did, and saw what she meant. Everywhere in town was dark. Not just the police station. Every electric light was out. The buildings, the streetlights, the lamp posts in the park. It was a complete blackout.

Except for the Town Hall.

Up the street, floodlights on a manicured lawn shone up at the brick building with its white columns. More lights on the

GHOST STORY

building lit up the front doors and the windows, and the clock in its front roof that was forever stopped at 11:59.

Darcy pushed the button on her little watch to light up the dial. It was ten o'clock. Two hours to midnight.

The streets were empty. That was unusual even for the sleepy little town of Misty Hollow. People should still be out in the park, or walking their dogs, winding the day down before heading home. It was like everyone knew not to be out of their homes tonight, that something wicked was not only coming their way but was already here.

"We have to do this now," Darcy said.

"Yeah," he agreed. "Yeah, I think you're right. You need your things first though, right?"

"Right."

"Bookstore?"

"Bookstore."

They were practically in front of the Sweet Read bookstore as it was. Getting there involved Jon pulling the car to the curb and shutting off the engine.

Then they sat where they were, staring out at the night.

"Is it safe?" Jon finally asked.

No, she wanted to say. They had to do this, though. "Won't know till we try, I guess."

After a long count of five seconds, Darcy took a breath, held it, and raced out of the car to the front door of her store. She yanked on the handle, expecting to fly inside with Jon right behind her.

Only, the door was locked.

Feeling stupid, feeling the rush of panic coming up inside of her, she turned to Jon with her hand out. "Keys. Quick."

Without hesitation he passed her his ring of keys, where the spare key to her store dangled next to his car keys and the key to their house and others. She was really glad she had insisted on him having a copy of his own.

Two seconds later they were inside and the door was shut and locked again. She turned to Jon, he turned to her, and as their eyes met she couldn't help but burst out laughing. They fell against each other, holding tightly, laughing, letting the stress of the past two days wash away.

"I love you," she told him.

"I love you, too. Now. Let's go send this ghost back to the eighteenth century."

Time was not their friend. Darcy had to remember that. "Okay. Wait for me here, will you? I need to get some things from the back. Watch the street and tell me if anything, uh, weird happens."

She could barely see his expression in the light from the waning moon, but if sarcasm had an expression, she knew this was what it looked like. "Right. Anything weird. Like a ghost causing a blackout or making an entire police force scared of their own shadows."

"Exactly. You know me so well." She kissed his cheek, then went to her office behind the checkout counter. She had to do it mainly by feel, until she got into the office itself and got the flashlight out of the top drawer of the desk. Switching it on, she sighed in relief that it worked. It lit up the entire space, pushing the darkness away. She had been worried that whatever influence Nathaniel Williams was exerting over the town's power would extend to things like flashlights, too. It didn't, apparently, and she could breathe easier knowing that at least something had gone right tonight.

"Millie?" she said quietly. "Are you here?"

GHOST STORY

Sweeping the flashlight beam around she caught a glimpse of a shadow in the corner wearing a long black dress, smiling an encouraging smile. When she swept the light back quickly the old woman was gone again. Just an impression of her spirit, enough to tell Darcy that yes, she was here to help.

"Good," Darcy said. "I understand what you meant by how things would get worse. They're a lot worse. I don't want anyone else getting hurt. I'm going to try an exorcism, but I could use you there with me."

There was no answer, and Darcy didn't know if that was a good thing or a bad thing.

"All right, then. Let's get what I'll need."

From one of the filing cabinet drawers she took out a square box of salt. Sometimes she and Izzy had to have their lunches here, when the workday was busy. She had pepper and a small bottle of soy sauce and a few little plastic packages of ketchup and, yes, salt.

Then from her bottom desk drawer she took out a small cardboard box, a duplicate of one she had put together to keep at home. No girl with abilities like hers could afford to be without one.

Her Emergency Communication Kit.

Calling a ghost to you and pushing one away from the mortal world might be two entirely different techniques, but they both involved a lot of the same gear. In this little box there were four tall white candles, matches because she'd learned the hard way you can't light a candle just by wishing for it, chalk, and plastic snack-sized baggies of sage, basil, garlic, and a few other household spices.

It didn't seem like much, but she was ready.

The book falling from the shelf up on the wall and landing with a thump startled her. The beam of her flashlight bounced in her hand and she very nearly dropped her container of salt.

"Millie!" she whispered. "Don't do that!"

It was Millie's own slim journal, and for it to have landed flat on its spine like that was impossible. The book didn't just fall open to a particular page. It fell, bounced open, and then flipped through several pages before settling on the one her aunt wanted her to see.

Darcy didn't get freaked out by these things anymore. In fact, she welcomed her aunt's advice in whatever form she could give it. Now, she looked down on a handwritten genealogy of the main families of Misty Hollow. The Graces, the LaCroix family, the Underwoods, and others. There were four full pages of these names. Darcy had read through them briefly on several occasions. She really couldn't care less who was related to who, but it was interesting to know family lines could be traced back that far. Like those parts of the Old Testament with all the begats that no one really paid much attention to.

This page had three of the major families on it. There were the Graces, the ones who Darcy and Millie were descended from. There was the Underwood's, a broken line that had yet to be filled in because so many of them had left Misty Hollow and never been heard from again.

The third family was a direct line from Roderick Chauncy. The leader of the original group of settlers who Nathaniel Williams had cursed for stealing the land out from under him. And then hanging him, of course. Darcy didn't know if that was how it had really happened or not but that was how Williams had seen it. That was why his spirit held so much hatred and why it was still tied here in Misty Hollow today.

Ghost Story

Darcy followed the Roderick Chauncy line, seeing the names change over the decades as marriages brought in new bloodlines, down through the years to the present day where one final name was listed in the ancestral progression.

Helen Nelson. The mayor of the town.

Of course. All the pieces were in place again. A direct descendant of the original group leader was now mayor of the town. Darcy was a descendant of the lawman who had hung Nathaniel Williams and she spent a lot of her time solving mysteries and putting bad people in jail, plus she was engaged to an actual police officer and her sister was one, too. Add into that the fact that land in Misty Hollow was now being sold off to various companies to bring new commerce into the town, and you had history repeating itself.

It was all happening again. The spirit of Nathaniel Williams had been stirring for a while now. Darcy was sure of it. All the bad things in town that had happened…she should have seen it. Even Chief Daleson commented on it. Things had gotten worse and worse here in Misty Hollow. Murder, kidnapping, and more. People doing bad things. Human beings at their worst.

Maybe the reason wasn't purely human, after all.

"Thanks, Millie," she whispered, before closing the journal and going back out to Jon. She knew who the real murderer was. She knew the reason the ghost had come out to cause havoc. She knew the method, and the way.

She was armed for the exorcism with both the proper tools and the proper knowledge.

It was time.

The Town Hall looked all the more eerie for being the only place in town still awash in lights. Jon followed her step for step, so close that his body brushed up against hers. Up the steps they went to the heavy double doors at the entrance. Darcy put her free hand on the left handle, and Jon took hold of the right. Her other hand held her box tucked carefully to her side. They looked at each other, serious expressions mirrored in each other's eyes.

"Ready?" Darcy asked him.

"Is no a choice?"

"Not really." She tried to smile at his feeble joke but it wouldn't hold. Taking a deep breath she firmed up her grip and counted, "One, two, three."

They pushed on the doors together.

They wouldn't open. They were locked after hours.

"Seriously?" Jon asked out loud.

"Maybe the back door?" Darcy offered.

"I'm not going to search all around this place for an opening that someone forgot to lock. There's no time for that."

"You have a better suggestion?"

Jumping back down the front steps two at a time Jon went to the front lawn, scouting around in the grass by the light of the flood lamps. When he found what he was after he bent down and scooped it up one handed.

As he got closer, Darcy could see what it was. A rock.

"You're going to break a window?" Darcy asked him.

"Well, we need to get in, don't we?"

"I know, but…you're a cop. A straight-laced cop." This time, she did smile. "I just never thought I'd see you breaking the law like this. It's kind of attractive."

He bounced the rock on the palm of his hand a few times. "I never knew you went in for the bad boy type."

GHOST STORY

"I fell in love with you, didn't I?"

Jon winked at her, cocked back his hand with the rock in it and aimed for the nearest window.

The doors unlocked with a loud, metal *snick* and swung inward.

Jon managed to hold onto the rock but couldn't stop his forward momentum. He ended up doing a windmill, barely keeping his balance, before steadying himself on his feet. Clearing his throat, he looked ruefully at the rock and then let it drop. "Well. Guess my bad boy moment will have to wait."

"It's okay," she told him, lifting herself up on her tiptoes to kiss his cheek. "I still think you're cute. Now. Let's go exorcise a ghost."

Even though the outside of the building was all lit up, the lights inside were at a muted low burn, like a brownout. They made their way forward slowly, ready for something or someone to pop out at them. Nothing happened. They made their way without any problem past the assessor's office and a janitor's closet, and other rooms besides.

"Where are we going?" Jon whispered. He had his hands held up like he was ready for a fight. "Do you have a location in mind where you want to do this?"

"I was thinking of Helen's office," Darcy answered in the same hushed tones. "I know I've felt Nathaniel Williams in there. His presence, I mean. And I'm sure that Helen has been speaking to him in there. It seems like the place to start."

"Darcy?"

"Yes, Jon?"

"Why are we whispering?"

She blinked, and realized how foolish they were being. The ghost would hear them whether they whispered or not. She was glad that the lights were humming low so that Jon wouldn't see her face turn red. "It seemed like the thing to do, I guess."

At the end of the hall was a T intersection. The hallway went left and right but in front of them was the door to Helen's big office. "Mayor" was spelled out in black lettering on the frosted glass. There was no way of seeing what—or who—was inside. They listened, but heard only silence.

"Think this one will be locked?" Jon asked her.

"Probably. Did you bring your rock?"

Jon's phone rang in his pocket, loud in the silence, and Darcy had never seen him jump that high before.

Trying to laugh, cough and breathe all at the same time, Jon took the cellphone out of his jeans and finally got the answer button pressed. "So much for being stealthy," he muttered.

"So much for your bad boy image, too," she teased.

He stuck his tongue out at her before putting the phone to his ear. "Hello, Grace. Now isn't really a good time…"

Grace's voice was a muffled shout on the other end of the line. Jon's face fell flat and he began pacing back and forth. "Yes, that's a safe bet. We'll watch for her. How's Andrew? All right. Call an ambulance for him. We'll keep you posted on our end. Right."

Darcy was on edge by the time he hung up and put the phone away. Well. More on edge than she had been. "Jon, what's going on? What happened to Andrew?"

He dropped his voice to a whisper again. "Helen clubbed him on the back of the head with that tall glass vase we had in the living room. Then she ran out of the house."

"Oh, no! You can't be serious? How is he?"

"Grace says he'll be fine. She couldn't say the same about the vase."

GHOST STORY

Darcy could not imagine Helen doing something like that. Was it because of the phone call Jon had made, telling her that the police suspected her of the murder? Why would she run? She should have stayed there at Darcy's house. That's where she was safe.

"We need to do this quickly," Jon told her, in a voice so low that she could barely hear it. "Are you ready?"

"I guess. Why are we whispering again?"

"Because I'm pretty sure I know where Helen went," he said, reaching for the office door.

It dawned on her what he meant. Of course. Once she understood, she kept her voice down as well. "You think she's here."

"I do. In fact I'm certain of it. Just be ready for anything."

"You mean, like a homicidal ghost drawing us into a trap?"

His eyes narrowed, and he nodded. "Yes. Exactly like that. Here we go."

He turned the knob on the door. It squeaked once but it wasn't locked. Silently counting to three, bobbing his head for each number, he threw the door open and they both rushed inside.

Helen's largish desk sat silently brooding under its thin plexiglass top. The desktop computer that took up one whole side of it was turned off. Book cases lined most of the walls, except where the three foot square painting of the beach hung, and where filing cabinets stood like short and squat sentinels watching them storm the empty room.

No one was here.

"Okay," Jon said, "I guess that's a little bit of luck for us. You want to set up while I keep watch?"

He was so handsome in the low light, her brave protector, offering to defend her when he didn't have his gun or even so much as a wooden stake. No natural ability to see or communicate with ghosts, either. That didn't matter to him. He would stand by her to his dying breath. She loved this man. She always would.

Putting her box on the desk Darcy opened it and began to take things out. "You know, we could elope. I guess. If you want to."

"What?" he asked, standing in the doorway and trying to look both ways down the hall at the same time. "You're serious?"

She nodded, biting her lower lip. She had always wanted the big, beautiful wedding that every little girl dreams of as a child. The thing was, she'd already had that with her first husband, Jeff. That hadn't ended well, for either of them. Now she was grown up enough to realize she didn't need the big ceremony with all of the trappings and fanfare. All she needed was Jon in her life.

"Darcy…" he began, then stopped. "I don't know what to say."

"Say yes?" she suggested.

"Hey, wait. I already proposed to you."

"You call that a proposal?"

She smiled as she said it, but she knew she was only talking to distract herself from what she was about to do. This was crazy scary and talking to Jon made it easier. He was more than just a hand to hold or a warm body to snuggle up to at night. He was good for her soul.

They were good together.

If it would make him happy, and make her happy, then she would get married in a paper sack.

"You want me to propose again?" he asked.

"A girl can never get too much of that sort of thing." She checked the candles over to make sure they weren't cracked and that their wicks were free of the wax. Good. Once she made the circle, they could begin.

"You want me down on one knee every night?" Jon asked, his grin lopsided in the near darkness.

"Maybe I do," she said, sticking the matches into her pocket and gathering the candles up into both hands. She winked at him.

"Well, maybe I—" His smile fell away and he looked off down the hallway. "Wait. What was that?"

Darcy stood very still in the middle of the room, juggling candles and spice packets, straining her ears for any sound. "I don't hear anything."

He sucked at the inside of his mouth for a moment, then nodded once. "I'll go check it out. You stay here."

"Jon, no!" she protested. "You can't leave me alone. Not here!"

"I can't let someone sneak up on us, either."

She knew who Jon meant by "someone." If Helen was here, there was a good chance Nathaniel Williams had gotten to her again, somehow. They needed to know about it, sure, but Darcy did not want to be left alone in the creepy Town Hall with the creepy ghost who might just creep up on her at any moment.

"Jon." Darcy managed to put a world of argument into that one word.

He came over to her, and hugged her carefully around the candles, and kissed her cheek. "Two minutes. I promise I won't be any more than two minutes. If I see Helen, or anyone else, I'll call for you. Okay? Stay in here, keep the door locked, and set up the communication ritual thing. I'll be right back."

Before she could argue it any further, he was gone.

Clenching her teeth, she took just a moment to settle herself, twisting the antique silver ring around and around her right ring finger. She felt the intricately carved designs, the impression of the perfectly shaped rose against her fingertip. For years she had worn this ring, spun it around her finger just like this whenever she was nervous or scared, letting it bring her comfort and strength. She had never known what it really was. A perfect representation of the way of exorcism. The way to send an evil spirit from this plane of existence into the realm of the dead for good, and block them from coming back.

Forever.

With a deep breath she made herself turn away from the door and begin setting up for the ritual. The candles went into their little holders, made from metal screw-top jar lids. Each lid had a hole punched into the center just big enough for the candle to wedge through. Her other kit, back at her house, had fat candles but these long ones lasted longer and there was less chance of the wick getting swallowed up into the melting wax. The holders had been her own idea, and they worked great.

Arranging the six candles into a circle on the floor in front of the desk, Darcy used the bags of basil and sage, and the box of salt, and very carefully laid out intertwining lines of each spice. There was just enough of the salt, and Darcy was glad of that, but it also meant she would only have the one chance at this. Leaving and coming back to try again wasn't really an option.

She checked her watch. The smiling face of the cartoon pony irritated her. It was too humorous and right now she wanted to be serious. Tomorrow, Darcy promised herself, she would get a different watch. This one had been a gift from Izzy's daughter, so she would set it aside to still wear sometimes, but she needed something that suited her better.

The time was eleven fifteen. It was late, and getting later.

It was also four minutes since Jon had left her here.

Ghost Story

Swallowing, trying not to put too much thought into that, she sat down cross legged in the middle of her circle with a match in one hand. Jon would be back soon. It was a large building, after all, two stories tall plus a basement that Darcy herself had never been in. It would take a while for Jon to look through every room.

She lit the first candle on her right.

Besides, he was a big boy now. He could take care of himself.

The second candle, and the third.

Not that Darcy couldn't take care of herself, too, she just would have felt better if Jon had been here to watch over her while she entered the exorcism.

The fourth candle, and then the fifth.

The last of the candles was behind her. With a deep breath, she turned where she sat, using her off hand to support her weight as she leaned in with the match.

"Darcy!"

The shout echoed through the halls like a thunderclap, an impossibly loud thing that almost had a life of its own. She startled as it slammed into the door to the office and made the walls shake and the match fell from her hand, extinguishing in the line of salt circling her.

She was on her feet in the next instant, carefully out of the circle with its five burning candles. The other matches were still in her pocket but she was stuck now. She couldn't extinguish the already burning candles because she couldn't stop the ritual once it started. And she couldn't light the sixth candle because there wasn't time.

That hadn't been Jon's voice calling to her. It had been Helen's.

Chapter Ten

It hadn't actually been Helen's. It had been mostly hers, but it was like her voice had been mixed together with someone else's. A masculine voice with jagged edges to it that cut against her ears.

Darcy swallowed, her throat suddenly dry and tight. Her mind raced in a thousand different directions at once. Where was Jon? Why was Helen here, and why was she calling for Darcy? What was that other voice talking through Helen?

Well, she actually knew the answer to that one. Nathaniel Williams had ahold of Helen again, using her as his personal mouthpiece, and maybe worse. If Helen had been taken over—again—then Jon could be in serious trouble.

Darcy left the circle as it was, careful not to disturb the curving lines of salt and spice as she swept out of the office into the hallway, looking up and down the short passageways. She wasn't very familiar with the layout of the Town Hall. To her left there were a few minor offices and the stairs the led to the basement, she thought. Way down to her right was the main room where all of the town meetings were held. Ahead of her the entryway doors beckoned.

Which way, she asked herself over and over.

Which way?

GHOST STORY

"Jon?" she called out for him. "Jon! Where are you?"

Laughter flowed through the halls, a mocking and coarse sound, made up of Helen's voice and that other combined. "Jon can't answer you right now, Darcy. Why don't you come down here and see for yourself?"

The voice was coming from the hallway on her right. She raced down to the door at the end, not worrying about traps or tricks, even this close to Halloween. Nathaniel Williams wanted her to come to him. He wanted her and Helen together to wreak his revenge. He'd told them to leave Misty Hollow or there would be more death. Darcy just hadn't realized the deaths he meant would be theirs.

If Darcy had anything to say about it, they wouldn't be.

The door at the end was already open, all the way open, and the lights in the room inside shone brightly instead of on low dim like the rest of the building. They illuminated a wide space that usually was filled with row after row of folding chairs. Tonight, it was empty. A low stage at the far end was where the mayor would stand behind her podium and tell the townspeople all about the important events affecting them.

Helen stood there now, without her podium, arms spread wide. Beneath her, on the floor below the edge of the stage, Jon lay sprawled on his side. His back was to her. She could see a dark stain of red at the collar of her shirt, at the base of his skull, but she couldn't see his face.

She heard herself gasp, and took two quick steps toward him.

Helen moved one hand, just a few inches, and a soft blow like some big invisible slap rocked Darcy back. The air, she realized. Helen had forced the air itself to collect and swirl and strike at her. No, not Helen. The ghost within her. The Pilgrim Ghost was having his fun.

"Helen, why did you come back here?" Darcy asked, inching her way forward instead of running, hoping that the ghost would ignore her long enough to get close, or that she could distract Helen enough to break his hold over her. "Why didn't you stay at the house where you would be safe?"

"I couldn't," Helen said miserably, in her own voice, her face slack even as her eyes sharpened. "He was calling to me. I could hear him in my mind, over and over, telling me that I had to come here."

Darcy cursed at herself. She should have thought of that. She should have realized. Helen had played host to Nathaniel Williams. Possibly for a very long time. His spirit would have ingrained itself in her mind like ruts in a muddy road. He would be able to communicate with her now over vast distances, even across barriers meant to keep him physically out of places. For that matter his spirit could have stood right outside one of the windows at Darcy's house and yelled into Helen for as long as it took to get her attention.

"Helen, I'm so sorry. I should have protected you better. I should have kept you safe." Darcy shuffled forward just a little bit more, hardly moving at all. "You need to trust me now. You need to listen to my voice, okay?"

"Stay where you are!" Helen's auto-tuned mix-up voice said. "Do not come any closer. Your boyfriend won't be hurt if you do as he says. He doesn't want Jon. He wants us. He wants me, and he wants you."

Darcy concentrated on breathing for a full ten count. "Helen, you know you don't want to do this."

"I don't want to do this," Helen agreed, her voice a little bit more her own again when she said it. "I don't want to. I don't…

GHOST STORY

have any choice. He's making me, Darcy. I don't have any choice. I...I'm sorry."

Tears spilled over and coursed down Helen's cheeks. Darcy knew her friend was still there. Helen was still in control, at least a little. Probably more than she realized.

Taking one more step was a risky gamble. Darcy took that gamble.

"Stop!" Helen screamed, making the fluorescent lights overhead on their metal supports shake and sway. "I'll hurt him, Darcy. I don't want to, but I will."

"He can't make you do that if you don't want to," Darcy pleaded with her friend. She was frantic now to get to Jon. Obviously, no matter what Helen promised, he had already been hurt. Obviously, Helen had done that hurting. She needed to protect him. "Don't do this, Helen."

"I have to," she said again, more tears flowing. "He says... he says if we offer ourselves to him he'll let it end with us. His revenge will be over. No one else will have to get hurt. If we don't...then he'll hurt everyone. Starting with Jon."

"Helen, why? You don't have to do this!"

"Yes I do! I don't have a choice. I've already committed murder!" Helen's body began to shake. Her hands came forward, towards Jon's motionless body. The temperature in the room dropped until Darcy could see her breath frosting and swirling in currents of air that had no source. "He told me. He told me what he made me do. I know what I am! I'm his. I'm lost. I'm a murderer, Darcy. He made me kill that poor girl!"

Bonnie Verhault. Dead on Helen's lawn.

That wasn't the whole story, though.

"Helen," she said, "listen to me."

"No! I know what I did. I know what I did!"

The ghost was telling Helen just enough of a lie to make it sound like the truth. Just enough to keep his control over her.

Darcy knew the truth.

The real truth.

"No, Helen. That murder wasn't done by your hands. Do you hear me? I know who killed that woman, and it wasn't you."

Helen's eyes blinked rapidly, like she was coming out of a pitch black room into the light, adjusting to the sudden illumination. More of herself, her own spirit, came to the surface. Her expression changed and twisted. "Darcy...? What?"

Darcy dared another step closer. "You didn't do it, Helen. It wasn't your hands that Nathaniel Williams used."

The air in the room swirled and built up into a physical push that rocked Darcy nearly off her feet. At the same time, it lifted Helen off the floor, holding and suspending her a full foot or more off the stage. "Shut up!" she screamed at Darcy. "You don't know anything!"

"Yes, I do." Darcy had to brace herself and push into the wind to keep from falling over. No small feat, since it kept changing direction, tearing at her from this side or that side. From behind. From in front. "Helen, it wasn't you. Do you hear me? I know you're actually here. I know Nathaniel Williams isn't in complete control of you. You're my friend, Helen! Listen to me!"

"How do you know?" Helen asked, even more of her own voice in the words now. She was coming out of her trance, thanks to Darcy's constant prodding. Out of the control of the Pilgrim Ghost. "How can you know that? You can't know!"

"I do," Darcy promised. "I know. You didn't kill Bonnie Verhault."

"Then who?" Helen demanded in a screeching wail.

GHOST STORY

"She did it herself, Helen. Bonnie Verhault stabbed herself to death!"

Helen's eyes widened. Color came back into her skin and for a moment, she was herself again. Only her.

Nathaniel Williams had lost his grip on her. At least for now.

Darcy knew it might be her only chance. She ran to Jon and knelt by him. He was breathing. That was what she noticed first. She sobbed in relief to know it, and then she rolled him on his back, careful of his neck, to try and wake him up.

He moaned, and his hands spasmed once, but then he was still again. She couldn't leave him here. She had to get him out. But how?

"Darcy."

Looking up she saw Helen at the edge of the stage. Her eyes had no focus. Her expression had gone slack again and Darcy knew her friend was lost back into the grip of the Pilgrim Ghost.

"Help me," Darcy begged her, hoping to reach through to her once more. She had gotten her arms under Jon's, and she planned on carrying him all the way out of the Town Hall all by herself if she had to. Dragging him, was more like it. Still, she wasn't looking forward to having to do that under the murderous eyes of Nathaniel Williams. "Helen, please, I know you're in there. Help me!"

The moment hung suspended between them as Darcy tugged and pulled and managed to move Jon ten feet toward the door. Helen stayed where she was, watching, her mouth working to say words that would not come out.

The air in the room stirred again, circling, coiling, plucking at Darcy's hair and clothes as it passed her by, slowly building stronger and stronger, flowing like the mists that snaked their way through the town in its darkest moments. Tension was mounting at the back of Darcy's skull like an invisible hand grabbing ahold of her to twist her emotions.

Three more feet. Four, maybe. The door still seemed so far away.

"Helen, help me!" she cried out, panicked and scared for both herself and for Jon. "You don't have to let him do this!"

Silently, Helen shook her head. Slowly, at first, but then faster, and faster, until she was practically spasming.

Then she stopped.

Staring at Darcy she said one, single word.

"Run."

Darcy was finally at the door leading out of the room. Jon was so much dead weight in her arms. The tumult in the room was building and expanding outward, the lights dimming further and then coming back up, the wind whipping past her to howl down the hallway with a banshee's moan. She took what Helen had said as the threat it was meant to be. There was no reason to think it was anything but.

Run, the ghost of Nathaniel Williams had told her. She had every reason to do exactly that. Every reason, save two. Jon, and Helen.

Darcy would not let this monster kill her friends. She had to do something to save them. The ghost wasn't interested in Jon. Helen had told her so. It was interested in the descendants of the men who had killed him. It was interested in her and Helen.

Sweating, breathing heavily, cold fear twisting her belly into knots, Darcy knew what she had to do.

Propping Jon up with his back against the wall in the hall, stealing a quick kiss, she began walking backward. Away from the meeting room. Away from Helen, and away from Jon.

GHOST STORY

It was what she had to do, if she was going to get the ghost to focus on her.

"Hey, Williams!" she called out. It came out as a frightened squeak, and she cleared her throat to try again. "Nathaniel Williams! You want me? Come and get me!"

Then she turned and ran as fast as she could.

All the way down to the mayor's office she raced without looking back. At her heels the wind hissed and grabbed at her, trying to hold her or tear her leg from its socket or snap the bones in her ankles.

An impossible thing for wind to do, except it was doing it anyway.

She made it to the door and grabbed at the handle and turned it and pulled and yanked on the door and slammed her fist against it and cried out in frustration when it wouldn't open until she remembered it opened in, not out.

The wind struck her across the back as she got it worked out and the extra shove pushed her into the room, pain blossoming across her shoulder blades. The strike was harsh enough that she reached back to feel for blood, sure she had been cut to the bone.

Her fingers came away dry. No bleeding. Her shirt was torn but that was all. She'd lucked out.

The wind continued to lash out and swirl and gust and the candles still burning in their holders were in danger of being blown out or knocked over and Darcy did not want to start this ritual all over again. She wasn't sure the Pilgrim Ghost would allow her to get even this far with things next time.

There couldn't be a next time. This had to end now.

Using her back and pushing with her legs she was able to force the door closed, and lock it, as the cutting voice of Nathaniel Williams flowed down the hall to taunt her. "Where are you going to run, Darcy? I have your friend. I have your fiancé. I hold the cards. Come to me. Come to me now and I might spare their lives in exchange for yours."

Darcy ignored him. He was a ghost. He could not hurt her.

That was what she kept telling herself, ignoring the more rational side of her brain that pointed out one girl was already dead, forced into it by a ghost who couldn't hurt her.

Only, it had.

"Darcy?" the voice called, sounding closer.

Digging into her pocket, Darcy sat down in the circle of salt and spice and flame. She crossed her legs. She closed her eyes and took a deep breath.

"Darcy!"

Then she took another match out of her pocket and turned to the last candle.

"Don't you make me come in there!"

A loud thump against the door made it shake in its frame as she lit the last of the six candles.

The circle was complete. Turning inward to herself, tapping in to a little bit of her own energies—a tiny piece of her soul—she reached out for Nathaniel Williams. His presence was everywhere here in the Town Hall. The place was saturated with his spirit. Finding him with her sixth sense wouldn't be the problem.

Forcing him off this mortal sphere would be a different matter entirely.

The door crashed inward with a heavy bang just as Darcy slipped into the inbetween space that hovered between the worlds of the living and the dead. The winds rushed at her, grabbing, tearing, whispered noises that could have been curses directed at her life and her sanity.

GHOST STORY

That coiling mass of air struck with the sound and force of a thunderclap but it never touched Darcy. It slammed into the invisible barrier, the expression of her own spirit, created and held in place by the completed circle.

It was the last thing Darcy heard before she lost all contact with her senses.

~

In her mind she envisioned a dark landscape. A flat surface with nothing on it except her, sitting cross legged like she had been in the circle of candles. Those came into existence next, one at a time around her, their flames unnaturally motionless like they had been frozen in time.

Then Darcy added the mists.

Rolling across the emptiness came the billowing curls and tendrils of white fog that she always used as a mental backdrop for communing with the spirits. It wasn't real, just like nothing here was real, but it helped her focus and gave her a surface to project her thoughts onto. Spirits came and went in the mists. They could find her, and she could find them.

Today, the usual clean feeling of her mental landscape was tainted with dark colors of filth and corruption. Something was tainting her connection to the spirit world. She knew what it had to be. It was the same thing that had kept every other ghost away from her perception for the past few weeks.

All of them, except Great Aunt Millie. She could never be forced away from Misty Hollow. Not while Darcy was still here.

Not even by the Pilgrim Ghost.

"Show yourself," Darcy said into the gloom. Her voice fell short, the dank fog absorbing the sound and keeping her isolated. "I know you're here already. You wanted me, I'm here. Show yourself."

It wasn't silence that met her words. It was the impending presence of something foul and evil.

Sitting up straighter, Darcy clenched her hands into fists on her knees. "I said, show yourself!"

A rushing presence like a collection of pure black force slammed into her from behind, knocking her forward to her hands and knees. Darcy gasped, throwing her arms forward to keep herself from falling flat on her face in a place where there was no physical reality to anything. Even so, it still hurt.

Two of the candles in the circle were knocked over, their little flames suddenly very animated.

The presence coalesced in front of her, dark matter forming a shadow that blurred and smoked and slowly became a distinct shape. A person, wearing dark trousers and a plain white shirt with string ties at the neck and puffy sleeves. Boots that went up to his knees clumped against the imagined floor of Darcy's conjuring. Sharp angles gave his face the appearance of chiseled pride, and his eyes were dark and brooding under a length of black hair held back in a short tail.

Nathaniel Williams bent over at his waist, his hands held together behind his back. He regarded Darcy with his head cocked to the side. "Well, well, well," he said in a pinched accent, his smile twisted and sardonic. "Thou hast some skills, at the least."

"Enough to take care of a murdering dead man like you," Darcy spat at him as she scrambled back to her feet, putting distance between them.

Williams chuckled and stood up to his full height, six feet tall and then some. Winds swirled through the mists around him whenever he moved. "Murdering dead man?" he repeated. "That was the best thou couldst manage?"

Deep breaths, Darcy reminded herself. Don't let the ghost-figment-of-your-imaginary-world bait you into doing something stupid. You're in control.

The winds buffeted at her, pulling her, pushing her, rising to a fever pitch, but she was in control.

Repeating that, over and over, helped her to calm herself down. I am in control, she said. I am in control. I am in control.

She was in control.

Do the ritual, said a voice whispered faintly on the roaring winds. *Start it now.*

How her Aunt Millie had managed to get through to this place that Darcy had conjured was impossible to say. Her words gave Darcy the push she needed, and with her aunt's strength added into her own, she locked herself into her struggle with the Pilgrim Ghost.

"Desirest thou to fight with me?" he asked her, walking in a circle around where she stood. "Marvelous! I should like thou to be demoralized before I kill thee."

Darcy thrust a hand forward, grabbing at his energy, mentally trying to make him yield to her. It was like trying to hold an ocean's worth of water in her arms as she extending her own spirit, enfolding it around his, wrapping him into her. Or, trying to at least. She felt him twist, saw the look of surprise on his face that she would be able to do that to him, and then saw his expression turn ragged with hatred.

"Get off me!" he shouted, throwing up his arm like a blade cutting through the mental ropes Darcy had entangled him in. His words were like knife thrusts of their own, sharp and abrupt and painful.

His spirit struck at hers, and she lost her grip on him entirely.

The world around her turned upside down and for a moment she was sure there was no up and no down. Until she found herself on her side and sliding with her feet up over her head. Then she was very sure there was a down. The pain lancing in long lines through her spine and ribcage told her there very definitely was a down.

"Don't worry, Aunt Millie," she groaned softly. "All part of the plan."

She just wished the plan didn't hurt so much.

"How quaint," Williams sneered, circling her again, slowly. "Thou callest upon the spirit of thine aunt? I knew her. Not well, of course, but enough to know she couldn't have beaten me either. She can not help thee. No one can. Death comes for you this day, Darcy Sweet. I need not even lift my hand."

He leaned into her, his face hovering over hers, the light in his eyes painful to look at. "I need not lift my hand, but I shall nonetheless."

His hand rose up in a fist, and into it the mists collected and solidified and became a sharp edged dagger with a wicked curve to it. It was aimed for Darcy's chest, and if it came down she knew she would die. Even if this place wasn't real, her death would be.

The wind swirled around them at a gale force, gathering every scrap of Darcy's own conjuring, turning it into a tornado around them, and as Nathaniel Williams smiled down at her it all collected behind him into a funnel with the knife at its apex.

"Die, Darcy Sweet," he said in a voice full of heated desire and centuries old hatred. "Die!"

His arm came down with the knife, the mists following, racing to tear into her.

Ghost Story

A single word passed through Darcy's mind.

Now.

Holding up her right hand she concentrated on her Aunt Millie's ring. The ghost, the embodiment of all things malevolent in the town of Misty Hollow, gasped when he saw the piece of jewelry shining before him, shrieked when he realized what she had done, and tried to stop his forward momentum. He was too late.

The image of his body stretched and lengthened, sucked into the ring as Darcy watched, the horrid and fetid mists following after. There was no way that something so small could contain so much. Possible or not, her aunt's ring caught hold of the evil that was Nathaniel Williams and held him trapped within the way.

Darcy spasmed like someone had punched her in the gut. It was a lot to take in, more than she had ever tried to do before. Even forcing Nathaniel Williams out of her body hadn't taken this much mental and physical strength.

The method of exorcism was simple. First, chant the right words to create the rhythmic vibrations that opened the portal between the two worlds. She had done that, just now when she had told herself over and over, "I am in control." It didn't have to be those words. They could be anything that had the same meter and cadence. The book Aunt Millie had led her to—the one Nathaniel Williams had tried to keep her from seeing—had suggested using that phrase because of its positive energy.

Next, the doorway to the other side had to be opened forcefully, and held open. Most spirits of the dead went to the other side because they wanted to. Some needed a little help to go and were happy to take it. For those few ghosts who didn't want to leave the world of the living at all, the only way to get rid of them was by force.

The door was open and waiting for Williams. Now she needed to show him the way out.

Unable to make it to her feet, Darcy rose to her knees, keeping her focus on her ring the whole time. The Pilgrim Ghost was lost inside. Not literally, of course, but everything here was symbolism. With a little bit of her own spirit used as a push, Darcy moved Williams along the etched lines and intricate maze design around her finger. She tilted her hand this way and that, flipping it over, rolling it sideways, forcing him down the way against his will. She heard him railing against her, swearing and cursing, and she didn't take those curses lightly but it didn't matter anymore. When she got him where she wanted him, this would be done.

The wind rose up hard against her, lifting her hair straight up and stinging her eyes. As she blinked rapidly to clear her vision, she lost sight of the trapped spirit on her finger.

He laughed, a harsh and bitter sound, thinking he had won at the last moment. She caught her right wrist with her left hand, held it steady, focusing every scrap of energy she had left in her into keeping her hold on Williams' ghost.

"No way," she told him. "No way do I let you out to cause trouble in my town again. Misty Hollow belongs to the living. You need to go now."

Never! he shrieked in her mind. *I am eternal! I am Nathaniel Williams! I will have vengeance on the descendants of those who did me harm!*

"Not where you're going."

She concentrated, searching for him down along the way, reaching out to feel for him…searching…

And then she found him.

The little dark bit of energy was moving backward along the line of an angular arc, a line that intersected three others right there. Tilting her finger down, then up, moved him back into place.

Still he struggled, and fought, and used the winds against her. It was a struggle, and she was exhausted already.

With one final turn of her wrist, the spirit of the Pilgrim Ghost rolled down a last twisting curve and into the beautifully worked rose on the ring.

She felt his scream in her bones. It was a painful and terrified sound, the sound of someone who knew they were going to die…for good.

It almost made her feel sorry for him. Almost.

No. Not really.

The ring had been cloudy with the mists dragged into it with Williams' spirit. Now, at the end of the exorcism, it shone brightly. More brightly than mere silver ever could. It was a celestial light, a light of purity and peace, pulling the evil that was Nathaniel Williams to his final rest against his will, kicking and screaming against Darcy's spirit.

It hurt. A lot. She held on to the bitter end, feeling everything she had draining away from her. Everything that was left in her. If this didn't end soon, she might get sucked in, too, and be lost forever.

It was a price she was willing to pay. She didn't want to, but if that was what it took to keep her friends safe, then so be it.

Even as that thought came to her mind, the rose on the ring flared. It shone of its own accord, separate from the ring. It was a red light that Darcy saw, and as she watched the petals of the red rose blossomed to their fullest, like a living thing. Flecks of light lifted away from it, an effervescent glow, and Darcy knew she would never see anything so beautiful ever again in her life.

The light on the band slowly faded, ebbing away, leaving only the light of the rose. Then even that lessened by degrees until all that was left was the ring. A simple, beautiful silver band.

Nathaniel Williams was gone. Darcy had won against the darkness.

Collapsing face first against whatever passed for ground here, Darcy shook her head and managed a faint smile. "I am never, ever doing that again," she said. Then after a moment, she shrugged. "Well. Unless I have to."

Letting herself go, she drifted away from the endless depths of this in between space, slipping back to her real body, waking up slowly to the land of the living once more.

When she did, she smelled smoke.

Chapter Eleven

In her vision, while she had been locked in deadly mental combat with the Pilgrim Ghost, she had seen two of the candles in her circle knocked over. It turned out that was exactly what had happened.

She woke up face down on the carpet. Down here, there was still enough air to breathe, although it was getting smoky and hot even this low to the floor. Somehow Nathaniel Williams' spirit had managed to actually knock her body around. She ached all along both sides. Her spine felt like it had been bent backward. Her skull ached. Other pains hurt less, but still argued for her attention.

Putting her hand up in front of her face, she looked at the ring in wonder. It had been amazing to see what it could do. It kind of scared her now, knowing what it was. All this time she had worn it because it connected her to Aunt Millie. She never could have guessed that by giving it to her, Millie would one day save her life.

She coughed, and inhaled a harsh breath full of heat and little specks of ash. That was when she realized she was in the middle of a blazing inferno.

The mayor's office was on fire. The candles that she had so carefully set in place in their holders had been knocked down, setting first the rug and then the nice wooden furniture and then the books in their shelves on fire. She had lucked out when the fire spread to the back of the room first. It was a miracle that she hadn't died from smoke inhalation already, or from being burned alive.

Now that would have been a terrible thing to wake up to. Sensing it was still a possibility if she didn't get moving, she forced her wobbly legs to stand her up and she staggered to the door. It had been knocked off its hinges, and the edges of it were already being lapped at by flames.

Out into the hallway she stumbled, the smoke from the room behind her roiling up along the ceiling in all directions. She coughed again, wondering if she had time to get a fire extinguisher. Didn't the Town Hall have a fire alarm?

She looked for one quickly, shuffling quickly up the entry hall, sure there must be something like that near the main doors. If there was, she didn't find it. There was nothing to see except a round, white clock near the entrance that told her the time.

11:59pm.

That gave her a moment's pause, until a loud *whoosh* showed her that the flames had eaten their way out of Helen's office and were now hungrily feasting on the wood paneling of the hall.

Jon. Where was Jon?

Edging past the growing flames as fast as she could, she found him right where she had left him, near the door leading into the meeting room. He was awake now, and she could have cried tears of joy if the air wasn't so dry and smoky. She fell against him where he sat on the floor, throwing her arms around his neck. It was all she could do to manage that. She was exhausted. Completely spent.

"Darcy?" He blinked at her, feeling at the back of his head repeatedly. "What happened? Did we win?"

An involuntary laugh that she couldn't stop bubbled up from deep inside. It felt good, to know she was alive and that, yes, they had won. The Pilgrim Ghost was no more.

Behind her, something exploded with the sound of shattering glass.

Right. They were in a burning building. Tender moment later, save themselves from fire now. "Jon, we have to go. I'll tell you all about it later but right now we can't be here."

"Why?" he asked groggily, letting her help him to his feet, and helping her in turn. "What'd you do? Burn the place…down…"

His eyes widened as he looked down the hallway.

"Oh."

"Long story," she told him. "Just trust me right now when I say we have to go."

She put her shoulder under his arm, although it was a question in her mind which one of them was worse off. Together, they helped each other step by step down the hall, carefully watching the slow spread of the flames.

Until the wall next to Helen's office blew out in a gush of red and orange fire that rolled like a ball across the floor and up the wall on the opposite side.

They both stumbled back, realizing they couldn't leave that way.

Unfortunately, that was the way out. Darcy's mind put together what that meant in a split second.

It meant they were trapped.

"There must be a back door," Jon said, raising his voice to be heard over the crackling roar of the growing conflagration.

"I've never looked for one, but there must be something, right? A window or something?"

Darcy remembered being in the meeting room. There were no windows there. There was the wide open floor, and the low stage, and she did not want to die in a burning building when the outside world was literally three feet on the other side of the wall she was standing next to!

Jon suddenly dropped like dead weight to his knees. "Jon?" she asked in a panic. "Jon, what is it? Are you all right?"

He nodded, but his eyes looked blurry and his grip on her arm was weak. "I'm still a little out of it, I guess. I can't…um, think. Darcy…?"

She forced her weight under his arm again, and pushed with all her might to get him to his feet. He moved only because she helped him do it, and she had the sickening feeling that he was going to pass out again. Worse, she knew she would do the same thing if she stopped to rest for even a moment.

"Jon," she said to him, making sure he kept his attention focused on her. "You have to help me, okay? I need you to stay with me because I can't do this on my own and I need your help, all right? Are you listening to me? Jon!"

"I hear…you…" he said, right before his eyes closed and he sank back to the floor, unconscious.

"No!" Darcy yelled to no one in particular. "No! Jon, get up!"

He wouldn't answer her. His eyes rolled back into his skull and he twitched, but that was all the response she could get out of him.

The fire raced closer, devouring the aged wood and wall paneling. The molding along the ceiling and floor and doorways was consumed like fine delicacies and each bite brought the flames closer to them.

GHOST STORY

Frantically she took hold of him from behind, hands in his armpits, and dragged him along the floor into the meeting room. It was too much for her battered body to take, yet she did it anyway. She would do anything it took to save him. There was no other option.

The fire made it to the doorway when she was only five feet into the room. Darcy looked around, saw the walls and the stage and the ceiling and absolutely no way out at all. There had to be some way. There had to be!

"Darcy."

From behind the stage, where an alcove had artfully concealed a door, Helen Nelson stood with her hand out to them. She was ragged, her clothes torn and her hair a mess, but Darcy could see in her friend's eyes that she was herself again. The curse of the Pilgrim Ghost had been lifted.

"Darcy," Helen said, "bring him this way."

"I can't!" Darcy sobbed. "I can't, Helen. I don't…I'm not strong enough."

And then Helen was at her side, taking one of Jon's arms while Darcy took the other, and together they fled the burning structure as it came down around them.

⌒

Two long hours in the dark cellar as the Town Hall burned above them would always be one of Darcy's least favorite memories.

It had saved their lives, though. Her and Jon and Helen. Looking at it that way, she was grateful that Helen knew the back way down through the meeting room. The back door that led outside had been on the other side of the building, as it turned out, past where the worst of the fire was, so it was good that

Darcy hadn't wasted time looking for it. Helen had arrived just in the nick of time.

She just didn't remember why she was there.

Wrapped in a rough woolen blanket on the back of a fire truck, Helen shook her head again. "I remember going to your house for dinner, Darcy. I remember being worried about you and Jon and coming to find you here. But I think I must have taken a knock to the head inside or something because a lot of it is fuzzy. Or just not there."

Darcy figured that was probably a blessing for her friend. She didn't have to remember the more horrible parts of the last two days. Darcy would never forget them. She stood huddled next to Jon, the two of them sharing one blanket, silently communicating their love and support.

The EMTs had checked Jon out and declared it was just a bump to his head. He'd probably have more dizzy spells in the days to come, and there would be an awful knot there for a while, and an x-ray at the hospital over in Meadowood probably wouldn't be a bad idea, but for now he had been allowed to sign off from any treatment.

All of them had inhaled far too much smoke, but no one was really worried about that. The fresh night air was doing them good. What had worried the paramedics the most, was Darcy's bruises.

Her left side was a mosaic of purple and yellow. Both of her arms were covered in red marks, some of them looking suspiciously like hand prints. She was sore all over, but she figured she would live. The nice EMTs had chalked it up to having half of a building fall down around her before the fire department could put the blaze out. They insisted that she ride with them in an ambulance to the hospital to be checked out, and Jon had given her that look that said she had better do it or she'd never hear the end of it.

So, she had agreed to go. They would be leaving any minute, but for right now she got to cozy into the warmth of her fiancé and know that everything would be all right.

Firefighters and police officers and curious onlookers poked around the remains of the Town Hall. The far corner of it still stood, but the rest was a charred mass of support beams and red bricks that had fallen in on themselves. The roof that had stood over the entryway doors had come crashing to the ground and now lay at a cockeyed angle over piles of debris.

"I can't believe we got pulled out of that," Helen said, shaking her head. "Good thing I got here when I did, I suppose. I would hate to think anything would have happened to you two. What were you doing here, anyway?"

Jon pulled Darcy to her tighter. "We saw the smoke," was his answer. "We got inside just in time to be cut off by the flames. I'm really glad you were there, Helen."

She shrugged off the compliment. With a shake of her head, she muttered, "I just wish I could remember…"

A loud chiming cut off all other sounds around them. Then another, the sound tinny and out of tune, like a hammer striking a bent pipe. Another, and another. People all around them stopped and turned toward the source of the sound. They stared, some of them pointing.

Darcy counted each of the tones until they were done, twelve in all. Everyone stared at the cracked face of the old Town Hall clock, propped up at an angle amid the debris. It had been stuck with its hands pointing at 11:59pm for as long as anyone could remember. Now they had suddenly started moving forward, chiming out the witching hour even though it had already passed them by.

"That's creepy," Jon whispered.

"I'll second that." Darcy knew Nathaniel Williams was gone. She'd felt him go. She couldn't help but wonder, though, if his influence would ever be cleansed from the town entirely.

Two paramedics in stiff white shirts came up to her, rolling a stretcher between them. "Oh, guys," she complained. "Is that really necessary?"

It was, and they helped her on and strapped her in. Just as they were going to wheel her away, Chief Daleson appeared out of the crowd, asking them to hold on a moment.

"Jon, Helen, I want you to hear this," he said. "You too, Darcy. We just got a call from the state crime lab. I had asked them to put a rush on the fingerprints we found on that knife."

"What knife?" Helen asked.

Daleson didn't miss a beat. "The one that killed Bonnie Verhault. Guess whose prints were on the thing?"

"Well, I'm sure I wouldn't know," Helen said, turning to look down at Darcy. "I didn't kill her."

"Nope, you sure didn't," the Chief agreed. It was obvious how happy it made him to be able to say it. "Turns out, she killed herself. Stabbed herself to death, based on the fingerprint evidence. We figure that land deal she was negotiating was turning sour on her. Probably a lot of other stresses in her life, too, if she could kill herself that way. Dumped herself on the lawn of the town's mayor as some sort of crazy statement. Can you believe that?"

He looked from Helen, to Jon, to Darcy, the wind puffing out of his cheeks. "How come none of you seem surprised?"

GHOST STORY

"Darcy figured it out a little while ago, Chief," Jon explained. "Come on. I'll follow you down to the station. I'm sure there's a lot to do."

"You aren't kidding," the Chief grumped. "The lights came back on in town but now everyone is freaking out because of the fire, and that incident back at the station didn't help. That, and the fact that it's almost Halloween."

The incident down at the station that he was talking about had turned out to be a rookie officer shooting off his weapon during a power grid failure. Accidental discharge. At least, that was what the official report would say.

Taking her hand, Jon leaned down to Darcy and kissed her cheek. "I'll meet you at the hospital. They'll probably have you discharged before I even get there."

"Are you kidding?" she asked him. "The way I feel right now I'm going to have them admit me and keep me for a week."

For a moment his expression slipped and she could see the effort it was costing him not to cry. Darcy had almost died this time. He had almost died. Helen, too, and how many others? No matter how the Chief and all the other people in town would try to rationalize what had happened, Jon and she would always know the truth. The Pilgrim Ghost had possessed Bonnie Verhault, tormented that poor woman until she had committed suicide and placed herself on Helen's lawn. The same thing had almost happened to Helen. Not to mention how he had gotten into Darcy's body and spirit as well.

"I'll be all right," she promised Jon. "Things will be better now. You'll see."

Darcy had no doubt that Nathaniel Williams had been at the core of a lot of Misty Hollow's worst problems. How many good people had that one demonic spirit ruined? How different would things have been without him hanging around this town?

There was no way to know the answer to that one. The only thing they could do was pick up the pieces and move on. That, and be more careful in the future. If there had been one ghost hiding in the shadows of this town, there could be others.

"Sorry, folks, but we have to go," one of the EMT's said in a friendly but firm way.

Darcy didn't want to let go of Jon's hands, but she was already being rolled away.

As their fingers slipped apart he blurted out, "March twentieth. Okay?"

"What?" she said, straining to see him around the shoulders of the paramedic at the back of the stretcher. "What's March twentieth?"

"The day we're getting married."

She was momentarily struck speechless. They had tried everything to come up with a day for their actual wedding and failed each time. To her, it had felt like he wasn't really interested in a wedding at all. That was why she had offered to elope with him. Hearing him set a date made her heart leap in her chest.

"But…wait, wait. Why March twentieth?"

"Because it isn't Valentine's Day," he said, moving through the crowds of people with the stretcher.

"But it's so far away!" she complained.

With that lopsided smile of his that she loved so much, he made her a promise. "I'll wait for you."

The EMTs maneuvered the stretcher up into the ambulance, the metal supports collapsing under her as they locked in place. She had one last glimpse of Jon, then the doors to the ambulance closed, and she was on her way to the hospital. She was in pain, and exhausted, and even with all that she couldn't help the smile that came over her.

They had a date. They were getting married.

Her life was perfect.

-The End-

Don't miss another book by K.J. Emrick!

Subscribe to the mailing list at http://www.kathrineemrick.com/cozyregistration.html to be notified when the next books in the Darcy Sweet Mysteries by K.J. Emrick are available.

We promise not to spam you or chit-chat, and only make occasional book release announcements.

Once you are registered you will be notified of new releases as they become available. Also from time to time I will give away a free story or other free gifts and have competitions for the people on my notification list, so keep a look out for those. :)

About the Author

Strongly influenced by authors like James Patterson, Dick Francis, and Nora Roberts, Kathrine Emrick is an up and coming talent in the writing world. She is a new Kindle author/publisher and brings a variety of experiences and observations to her writing.

Based in Australia, Kathrine has wanted to be an author for the majority of her life and can always be found jotting down daily notes in a journal. Like many authors, she loves to be surrounded by books and is a voracious reader.

In her spare time, she enjoys spending time with her family and volunteering at the local library.

Her goal is to become a bestselling author, regularly producing noteworthy content and engaging in a community of readers and writers.

To find out more please visit the Kathrine's website at kathrineemrick.com

Made in the USA
Middletown, DE
26 March 2018